Zach couldn't believe he was thinking about marriage.

It wasn't something he'd ever thought about a second time. He was a pretty well-rounded dad, willing to do whatever was necessary for his kids.

But lately, he wasn't thinking of marrying just for the children. He wanted to do it for himself, as well.

He'd liked those nights he spent with Ginna. Not just the sex, but the cuddling, the conversation.

He never considered himself someone who thought in terms of hearts and flowers, but it was easy to think that way where she was concerned.

Personality of sunshine. A smile that made a guy just feel damn good. And a pair of legs that had him thinking some even better thoughts.

Yes, it was way past time for him to tell Ginna about Emma and Trey. Especially since he also had to tell her he was falling in love with her.

Available in July 2003 from Silhouette Special Edition

Two Little Secrets

LINDA RANDALL WISDOM

SILHOUETTE®
SPECIAL EDITION™

*Silhouette, Silhouette Special Edition and Colophon are
registered trademarks of Harlequin Books S.A., used under licence.*

*First published in Great Britain 2003
Silhouette Books, Eton House, 18-24 Paradise Road,
Richmond, Surrey TW9 1SR*

© Words by Wisdom 2002

ISBN 0 373 16920 5

23-0703

*Printed and bound in Spain
by Litografia Rosés S.A., Barcelona*

LINDA RANDALL WISDOM

is a Californian author who loves movies, books and animals of all kinds. She also has a great sense of humour, which is reflected in her books.

Many thanks to my agent, Karen Solem, for keeping me on track, for being there when I need her. You are very much appreciated.

Prologue

"Judgment for the plaintiff in the amount of five thousand dollars." The striking of the gavel backed up the judge's ruling. "Next time, madam, don't choose a man who lies even when truth hits him in the face. And, sir, you are lucky you're not in jail for the stunt you pulled."

"Yay, Ginna!" The cheers echoed in the room.

Ginna Walker strolled to the center of the hair salon and dropped into a deep curtsy. No easy feat, considering her narrow short skirt.

Now her voice echoed out of the speakers. "Naturally I am very happy with the judge's decision. The judge could tell he was lying about the money being his. The account was in my name only. He lied to bank personnel and cost that teller her job as a result. I just wish he'd been punished, too."

A man's surly voice was next. "I can't believe the judge believed that *bleep!* lies. That money was supposed to be in a joint account. The only reason that *bleep!* did this was because I have a new life and she's jealous."

Ginna laughed out loud.

"The man never stops. A so-called joint account that only carried my name on it. I still can't figure out how

Denny duped that teller into letting him clean it out," she told her friends and co-workers. "Could anyone remind me why I married such an idiot?"

"Because he had a cute smile and he reminded you of a puppy," Cheryl, one of the nail techs, said.

"Because you said he actually listened to you," Nora, one of the other hairdressers, put in.

"Because he sent you three dozen red roses on Valentine's Day," was added.

"Yes, but he used my credit card to pay for them," Ginna said ruefully.

"That was your first clue he was a total jerk," Sonia, one of the masseurs, piped up.

"I should have divorced him right there and then." Ginna picked up the television remote control and switched it off. "It would have saved me a lot of trouble."

Her friends kept pity from their gazes as they looked at her. They all knew exactly why there had been a divorce, but those sorrowful facts were neatly tucked away. It had taken a while before her smiles were spontaneous again.

CeCe, the elegant owner of the Steppin' Out Salon and Day Spa, rose from her chair and walked over to Ginna. She rested her hands on the younger woman's shoulders.

"Do not worry, my little Ginna. You will find a man who will see you as the treasure you are," she told her.

Ginna looked at her boss, who everyone considered ageless. She could be thirty. She could be sixty. The woman's beauty, Ginna thought, was the type that began from within. Anyone who worked for CeCe was considered a part of her family.

"Then if you say so, it will come true," she said

lightly. "But you don't mind if I wait awhile before the perfect man comes my way?"

CeCe's laughter was light and musical to the ear. "My dear, love doesn't come at your beck and call. You answer its call." She hugged her and stepped back. "Ladies, we have all this lovely champagne to finish," she announced.

Ginna walked over to the table laden with rich pastries, bottles of champagne and a lazy Susan holding various fresh vegetables with a dip nearby. She picked up a custard-filled éclair and bit into it.

The lounge for the Steppin' Out spa clients was a restful area with love seats and chairs that were designed for comfort, as well as looks. Exquisite paintings of European pastoral scenes hung on the walls. Many a woman enjoyed the plush feel of the mint-green carpet underfoot. The wide-screen television in one corner was encased in elegant walnut, used to play specially created videos showing the spa's amenities.

Since the spa was closed this evening, the employees took over the room to watch Ginna's television debut on one of the popular courtroom programs.

"Yes, but then you wouldn't have had your twenty minutes of fame on television," Phoebe, one of the spa's estheticians said, and busied herself with a nail file. Cheryl clucked her tongue, muttering about proper shaping as she took the file out of Phoebe's hand and finished the job herself. "Or gotten more than he owed you."

"If he hadn't out and out lied in court, she probably would only have awarded me the money he took," Ginna admitted. She dropped into one of the chairs in the salon and spun around. "He did it to himself."

"And what are we doing with the money?" Nora asked in a singsong voice.

Ginna grinned broadly.

"I am taking the vacation of my dreams."

"THIS IS A JOKE, right?" Zach Stone looked at the sheets of paper his sister had unceremoniously thrust into his hand.

"Do I look like I'm kidding?" She tapped the top paper. "Happy birthday, big brother."

"Lucie, my birthday's seven months away," he said dryly.

She shrugged off his statement. "Then think of it as two weeks in heaven. Sun, sand and surf. Maybe you'll even go wild and have a hot island romance. It wouldn't hurt you, you know."

"Romance?" He started laughing. "Lucie, I have two kids who will be starting kindergarten next year. My life consists of Big Bird and Elmo. Not spending my days on a tropical island beach."

"Then I suggest you start thinking about it, because you leave next week." She held up a hand to forestall the arguments she expected to hear. "Emma and Trey will be staying with us."

"Terrific. While I'm gone, Nick will teach Trey how to hack into a government computer, and God knows what will happen to Emma while her brother is in prison," Zach muttered in a dark voice.

"He hasn't done any of that for the last three months," his sister reminded him.

Zach thought about telling her he'd caught his eight-year-old nephew at his computer and the moment he was sighted the boy shut everything down. Zach had nightmares for a week about a member of a secret government agency coming knocking on his door.

He was positive the boy would run the country one day.

"Zach, you need to get away," Lucie said softly but forcefully. "You haven't done one thing for yourself since the twins were born. You need this."

"I took a vacation six months ago."

"Taking the twins to Disney World doesn't count," she argued. "As it was, you turned it into a working vacation by coming back with enough material for a few months' worth of your column. Fine. You want more material? Go to Hawaii and write about a single dad at a singles resort."

"I'll have plenty of time for myself when they graduate from college." He feared he was losing the battle. Lucie was like a Gila monster. Once she sunk her teeth into something, she didn't let go.

She shook her head. "It doesn't work that way. I planned this trip to give you everything you could ever want. Just pack up some casual clothes and suntan lotion and you'll be all set."

Zach got up and walked over to the patio doors overlooking the backyard. He watched his son and daughter playing tag with their cousin outside.

Since the day their mother died giving birth to them, he'd focused his life on giving them a rich full life in an attempt to make up for what they'd lost. By doing that, he'd pushed his own personal needs to one side. He couldn't even remember when he'd last gone out on a date.

He didn't want to take the trip his sister was generously giving him.

Maybe he should tell her to take the trip in his place, and he'd watch Nick for her. Maybe she'd even find a man who could handle the boy.

The offer hovered right there on his lips.

Chapter One

People were not meant to fly.

The previous day, Ginna had been scrubbed with sea salt, waxed, exfoliated, massaged, moisturized, moussed and polished. Her skin glowed and felt smooth as silk. Thanks to her co-workers' efforts, she was sent off to have the time of her life.

If only she didn't have to fly to achieve it.

Ginna Walker was known to be fearless. With three brothers, she'd had to be. Over time, she'd handled snakes, lizards and even a scorpion named Ralph.

But when it came to walking into a large cylinder that a human and computers navigated through the air, she didn't do as well. If it hadn't been so expensive, she would have opted for a cruise.

Except the movie *Titanic* stayed with her much too long.

So she'd armed herself with motion-sickness medication, a couple of paperback novels and a positive attitude to get her over the Pacific Ocean.

She made her way down the aisle to her seat. She pushed her carry-on bag into the overhead compartment, then settled herself in the window seat assigned to her. She opened her book and pretended not to hear the jet engines warming up or feel the faint rumble under her feet.

"Excuse me, I'm afraid you're sitting in my seat."

She looked up into a pair of brown eyes that rivaled Casper's, her German shepherd's.

"I don't think so."

He didn't move. "I do think so. You're in my seat."

She looked up at him, refusing to back down.

"This is seat 15C and my ticket reads 15C." She pulled her ticket out of her bag and showed it to him.

As if not to be outdone, he brandished a ticket with the same seat number printed on it.

She glanced at his ticket and smiled. "Amazing, my ticket says the same thing. Besides, haven't you ever heard of possession being nine-tenths of the law and all that?"

"I guess we'll need a third party to figure this one out," he said, pushing the call button.

The flight attendant was warm and helpful as she took both tickets to investigate. When she returned, she was equally apologetic.

"I'm very sorry, Mr. Stone, but somehow the same seat assignment was made for both of you," she told him. "As Ms. Walker's ticket was purchased first..." Her voice fell off. "I'm afraid we have no more window seats. In fact, we're full except for the middle and aisle seat here."

He nodded. "That's fine with me."

She handed them back their tickets and went about her duties.

"Sorry about that. I'm Zach Stone." He held out his hand.

"Ginna Walker." She felt his warm palm slide across hers.

Not bad at all. She judged him to be a couple of inches over six feet and nice-looking, with dark-blond hair she knew would lighten under the Hawaiian sun. It needed a good shaping, her keen hairdresser eye noticed. Soft yellow polo shirt, khaki-colored pants. A pair of glasses stuck out of his shirt pocket.

Maybe the flight won't be so bad, after all.

All the way to the airport, Zach had busied himself with instructions for Lucie about the twins. His sister looked at him as if he'd lost his mind.

Which he had. He was leaving his precious babies with his sister and her son, a child who aspired to be number one on the FBI's Most Wanted list.

"Nothing is going to happen to the twins," Lucie had said firmly, steering him through the security checkpoint and toward the gate. She held on to him as if she feared he would bolt in the opposite direction. "Emma always knows when Nick is trying to con her and she keeps Trey out of trouble. You just enjoy your vacation. And remember what I told you. For the next two weeks, no mention of your kids. You're a single man out for relaxation. That's it. And if you get lucky—" she paused "—I packed what you'll need in your shaving kit."

Zach groaned. He really should have made a run for it, but he knew his bloodhound of a sister would only drag him back. The woman was relentless.

He dropped into the aisle seat and adjusted his seat belt. He wouldn't be surprised if Lucie had stationed herself by the door, prepared to stand there until the plane left the ground. With him in it.

An exotic fragrance he couldn't hope to name floated from his seatmate. Nothing overpowering but enough to tempt the senses. The lady was ready for her vacation in the islands in a short black knit skirt that bared a pleasant amount of leg and a blue silky top that stopped a couple of inches short of the skirt's waistband. Brown hair that shone with gold and coppery highlights was pulled up and back in a curly ponytail that cascaded down her back. The eyes that watched him were a startling shade of blue. They were large and liquid, meant to captivate a man. Her voice held a husky note that was equally enthralling. Zach, the kid, would have stuttered his way through an introduction. Zach, the man, almost swallowed his tongue.

Maybe this vacation won't be so bad, after all.

Since his seatmate was engrossed in her book, Zach opened the book he'd brought with him. With Lucie so insistent on his finding some romance in the islands, he wasn't about to allow her to choose his reading material.

As they took off, he glanced out the corner of his eye and noticed her knuckles were white as she gripped the book.

"Flying's safer than riding in a car," he said in a low voice, in the hope of relaxing her.

"Cars remain on the ground while planes, which are infinitely heavier, go up in the air and have the chance of coming down when least expected," she murmured.

He noticed she started to relax once the plane had leveled off, even if one leg still had a habit of jiggling up and down. Which drew his attention back to her legs, which were as nice as the rest of her.

"Don't worry, I won't start screaming or anything," Ginna said. "I couldn't sleep last night, so I turned on the TV. Big mistake. I think every disaster movie ever made was on. I channel-surfed from crashed planes to earthquakes to tornadoes to sinking ships. You watch enough of those and anyone with normal intelligence would be afraid to leave the house."

"I guess that could get a person thinking," Zach admitted, silently amused by her candor. A logical man to the core, he couldn't imagine that watching a few disaster movies would keep him off a plane.

Ginna leaned over. "If I'd seen one more movie showing a plane crash, I wouldn't be here," she confided in a low voice. "I'm not a good flyer. When my mother was six months pregnant with me, she was on a plane that developed engine trouble and could have crashed. Which is why I usually spend my vacations at places you can drive to."

"That could limit your options," Zach commented.

Ginna shrugged. "I live in Newport Beach a short drive from the beach, a little over an hour's drive from the mountains, maybe a couple of hours from the desert. I think I have most of the bases covered if I want to get to one of those places. Anything else, I plan for a longer drive."

"Yet you're flying five hours to a Pacific island."

"I got a great deal from a client who's a travel agent," she said, then went on to clarify, "I'm a hairdresser."

"Funny, I got a great deal from my sister, who happens to be a travel agent," Zach said dryly.

Ginna raised her plastic glass of diet soda. "To travel agents who know where the deals are."

Zach tapped his glass against hers. "The plastic clink isn't as satisfying as crystal goblets, but we know the sentiment is there," he said.

She nodded. "Exactly. The thought is there. So what do you do, Zach?"

"I write a magazine column," he replied, figuring it was close enough to the truth.

"Really? Let me guess. A travel column. How to fly and arrive in one piece."

"Are you sure you don't write fiction in between haircuts?" he joked, relieved she'd answered her own question.

She shrugged. "I've been told I have an overactive imagination, but I can't even write a decent letter. I guess when someone says they write a magazine column, I tend to automatically think of the wilder side of the business. Someone who's free and easy, able to pick up and go when they please. And you seem to be a good flier."

"I was in Florida not all that long ago." He figured that was the truth without adding that his trip involved Disney World from a four-year-old's point of view.

"My parents took us there years ago. Did the Disney World thing. They had just as much fun as we did."

"We?"

She nodded. "I have three brothers and one sister. Keeping tabs on all of us wasn't easy. Mom once said if she could have, she would have hooked transponders on us so she'd know where we were at all times. Dad said if they lost one of us, it would just be one less mouth to feed. We figured he meant it."

"Close-knit family, then?"

"We're all pretty close in age and I guess we'd qualify as a gang. Makes family gatherings interesting," she said candidly.

"I just have the one sister," he said. "There're times when I feel as if she's three people in one."

As the flight progressed, Zach found himself enjoying this time with Ginna. He couldn't remember meeting such an open and honest person. The last lovely woman he'd talked to was the kids' pediatrician. He was relieved he could carry on a conversation with a woman without discussing eating habits and how best to handle a child's fears at night.

They made jokes about the airplane food served to them and discussed movies, books and even touched on current events. Zach was definitely enjoying himself.

So why is she looking at me the way a surgeon looks at a critically ill patient?

THIS IS EXACTLY *what I need. Time away from work and the attention of an attractive man.*

Ginna gave a start when she was positive the plane lurched in a way it shouldn't have. She relaxed when the pilot's voice came on and announced they would be landing soon. She was looking forward to planting her feet on solid ground again.

At the same time, she was reluctant to leave this small space with Zach.

She breathed another sigh of relief when the jet's wheels touched ground with barely a bump. They soon stood up and slowly filed down the aisle.

The moment they stepped onto the jetway she could feel the difference in the air and atmosphere. Zach walked by her side as they headed for the luggage carousel. He took her carry-on bag for her.

"I understand the hotel has a shuttle bus," he said, after learning they were staying at the same hotel.

"That's what I was told also," she replied.

"Why don't you call the hotel and request the shuttle to pick us up? I can watch out for the luggage if you tell me what yours looks like," he suggested.

"My nieces offered to let me use their Barbie suitcases, but I explained I needed something a lot larger."

She laughed. "It's a large teal soft side with a hot-pink band around it."

"I'm sure that will stand out."

Ginna found the phone and board listing the hotels. She made the call and was assured a van would pick them up in about forty minutes. When she returned to the luggage carousel, she found her suitcase at Zach's feet. He was occupied grabbing a black suitcase from the carousel and setting it down by his side. He looked up when she reached him.

"They'll be here in about forty minutes," she told him. "They pick up by the hotel shuttle sign, which is right outside."

Luckily the shuttle bus was prompt in picking them up and transporting them to the hotel.

"This is just what I needed," Ginna breathed, looking around the lobby with avid interest.

She was smiling and bubbly during check-in procedures. In no time, she was given her room information.

Ginna turned away to follow the bellman when Zach touched her shoulder and spoke her name.

"Have dinner with me tonight," he coaxed.

She tipped her head to one side as if considering his invitation.

"Nothing in small trays or plastic cups? I can have a drink with an umbrella in it?" she quipped.

"Anything you want," he said, meaning it.

"I'll meet you down here at seven," she replied with a smile that seemed to shoot right through his heart. She turned away again and followed the bellman.

When Zach turned back to the desk, the clerk looked at him with something akin to awe.

"Have a nice stay, Mr. Stone," he finally said as he handed the key card to the bellman.

He smiled. "I'm sure I will."

The minute Zach was alone in his room, he pulled out his cell phone and tapped out a familiar number.

"Donner residence. Come on over and we'll eat you for dinner!" a voice blasted.

Zach groaned. "Not funny, Nick. Where's your mom?"

"She's cooking dinner." The boy laughed uproariously.

"Let me talk to her."

"Honestly, Nick, you know your uncle doesn't have a sense of humor," he heard his sister saying in the background. Then she was on the phone. "Hey there, big brother. Is it as gorgeous there as they say?"

He walked over to the sliding glass door and pushed it open. The sound of waves crashing on sand and rocks was the first thing he heard.

"More so. How're the kids?"

"What? You think I locked them in a closet the second you were gone?" She chuckled. "They're fine. Emma's helping me make a salad and Trey's feeding Luther." Luther was the twenty-five-pound family cat that Zach estimated was older than dirt.

"Just make sure it's not the other way around." Zach was all too familiar with the cat's insatiable appetite.

"Zach! Listen to what you're saying. You need to relax. Now I know this vacation is the best thing for you."

"Luce, I can't just forget I'm a father," he protested.

"Of course you can't." She lowered her voice. "But there're times when you need to remember you're also a man. This is your chance, for a short time, to forget you're Emma and Trey's dad. Just be Zach Stone, free-wheeling single guy. Spend time on the beach, get a boogie board and ride the waves. And if you meet some-one in the process, even better.''

''You know what? I never want to know about any of the times you take off for one of your recharging weekends,'' he told her.

''I go to a spa,'' she said with a virtuous sniff.

''Yeah, that's what you tell me, but now I wonder if that's really what you do.'' He shifted the phone against his ear. ''Can I talk to the kids?''

''Emma! Trey! It's your dad!'' she called out.

''Daddy!'' Zach flinched as his daughter's excited squeal assaulted his eardrum. ''Aunt Lucie's lettin' me cook. But not on the stove,'' she assured him as if she knew his instinctive response to that announcement. ''I get to tear up lettuce for our salad. Don't worry, Aunt Lucie made me wash my hands first.''

''That's great, sweetheart.'' He found himself having to force the enthusiasm. He should be happy she wasn't pining away for the major man in her life. That she was enjoying herself. He talked to her a few more minutes before Trey had his turn.

''Luther makes really gross smells,'' he informed his dad, then went on to describe Nick's latest escapade.

''Okay, enough,'' Lucie interjected, obviously snatch-ing up the phone. ''All that happened was that Nick picked up the wrong can of cat food at the grocery store.''

''So they're doing fine,'' Zach said, sounding almost morose.

''Yes, they're doing fine. You know what you need to do? Shower off the trip, go downstairs and find a beautiful woman to take to dinner.''

Zach opened his mouth with the intention of telling her he was going to do just that, but stopped himself.

He knew his sister well enough to know that if he confided in her about Ginna, she'd insist on all the details.

"I'll see what I can do," he said. "Luce?" He paused. "Thanks."

"Anytime, big brother. After all, you've always been there for me," she said softly. "I couldn't have gotten through it all if it hadn't been for you." Her tone suddenly turned brisk. "So get out there and relive those wild times of your youth. And don't worry about the twins!" She hung up before he could say another word.

"Goodbye to you, too," he murmured, grinning.

Zach unpacked his clothing, put away his shaving gear and decided he had enough time for a quick swim before he needed to get ready for his dinner date with Ginna.

GINNA DIDN'T WASTE any time unpacking and hanging up her clothing. She made a trip to the vending machine and ice machine and fixed herself a glass of diet soda. With that in one hand and her cell phone and address book in the other, she walked out onto the balcony. She dropped onto one of the chairs and looked out over the ocean.

For several moments, she was content just to sit there and enjoy the serene setting.

"Oh, yes," she murmured. "Denny, this is the absolute best thing you ever did for me, you scum-sucking bottom feeder."

She switched on the phone and tapped out a series of numbers.

"Hello?" A woman's voice answered.

"Hey there, travel agent to the rich and famous," Ginna said cheerfully.

"I wish!" The woman chuckled. "So how's it going? Did I do good?"

"You did better than good," Ginna replied. "You are talking to one very satisfied client, and all I've seen so far is the lobby and my room. I braced myself for what I thought would be a flight from hell and, instead, met this great guy who took my mind off my fears. Let me tell you he was better than any over-the-counter medication. And he's invited me out to dinner tonight. Luce, you are a miracle worker."

Lucie Donner laughed along with her. She didn't need to be psychic to know her plan had worked. Both her brother and her friend sounded happy, which meant their meeting had gone well. Now she could only pray the rest of their vacation would be just as rewarding.

"What can I say, Gin? For the past five years, you've kept my hair looking great. When you were awarded that money from your lawsuit, you told me you decided it was time to do something for yourself. You wanted an out-of-this-world vacation—I figured the least I could do was make sure you got one."

Chapter Two

Zach was convinced he'd died and gone to heaven.

He had come downstairs ten minutes early. He spent some time in the gift shop, looking at bright-colored T-shirts and beach towels.

It was a man murmuring "Now that's what I call a woman" that first caught his attention.

He turned around in the direction of the elevators. He instinctively knew the man was talking about Ginna.

Nick would have called her a hottie. For once Zach wouldn't have disagreed.

Ginna had dressed for the warm climate in a silky cobalt-blue handkerchief halter top and a blue tropical-print ankle-length skirt. The high-heeled sandals she wore put her almost eye level with him. An exotic-looking white flower was tucked behind her right ear while her hair tumbled down her back in loose curls. Even with the sexy picture presented to him, all he could see was the intense blue of her eyes.

"When I look at your eyes, I feel as if I'm looking into the ocean," he murmured, walking up to her.

Her smile warmed considerably. "Why suh, I do declare you are flattering lil ol' me unduly," she said in a syrupy Southern drawl.

"Sorry, sweetheart, Scarlett O'Hara, you ain't." He grinned.

"Damn Yankee," she said, deadpan.

"Wasn't that a baseball movie?" Zach took her arm and tucked it under his.

"Flatterer and quick on the uptake," she said with a smile filled with approval. "I like that. Just don't think your charming and witty answer will get you out of my drink with an umbrella in it. I intend to order the fanciest drink they offer."

He inhaled the scent that drifted off her skin and at the same time noticed the shimmering glow on her bare shoulders.

As the hostess led them to a table on the lanai that overlooked the beach, he thought about the evening ahead. He didn't need a psychic to tell him this was going to be an evening he'd remember for a long time.

Ginna didn't disappoint him. She was warm and friendly to their waitress, discussed a variety of drinks and finally settled on one called Tropical Sunset. She was delighted that the drink not only sported an umbrella but a pineapple spear.

"There is nothing like the Hawaiian Islands," she confided as she nibbled on the pineapple. "The minute you step off the plane you instantly relax. You want to put on your bikini, slather on some sunscreen and just lie on the beach."

"I think I'd go for something that covers a little more than a bikini," Zach said. "I'm the modest type."

Ginna grinned. "Come on, Zach, tell me more about you. Likes and dislikes in foods, what you like to do on the weekends, any pets, where you go for haircuts." Her bright eyes sparkled with mischief.

"Hate broccoli and cauliflower, like squash and green

beans. Like to go hiking in the mountains when I can."
He doubted running after the kids at the local playground
qualified as a weekend activity. "No pets. A very nice
guy named Rupert cuts my hair every four weeks." He
grew suspicious at the look on her face. "What's wrong
with my hair?"

"Hate corn and lima beans, like green beans also, and
carrots. I have Casper, a white German shepherd, who
enjoys long runs on the weekend," she replied. "One
of my friends cuts my hair, and yours could use a good
conditioner and some shaping. Sorry, occupational haz-
ard. Rupert gives you a decent cut, but I can give you a
better one."

*Why did he feel as if she'd just suggested something
a lot more intimate?*

He was ready to give her an enthusiastic yes, but managed to remain silent.

She leaned forward. "Am I unnerving you, Zach? For
a minute there, you looked panicked."

"I think it's more panicking that I won't remember
how to relax," he said. "You seem to have it down to
a fine art."

"I work very hard. I realize some people think that
hairdressers are flaky individuals who don't understand
what work is. Trust me—" she lowered her voice
"—it's not easy standing there listening to a woman
explain just how she wants to look, while deep down
you know no matter what you do, there's no way you
can make her look like Heather Locklear. Explaining to
her what will work better for her is diplomacy to the nth
degree. But I love it. I love seeing women brighten up
when they leave the salon. I love knowing that my efforts help them feel beautiful."

"An artist," he murmured, finding himself just enjoying the sound of her voice.

"Artist?" She looked delighted with his description. "I can't draw a straight line with a ruler. I was the only child in my school's history to flunk fingerpainting. Although, unlike my brothers, I didn't stick the paintbrush in my mouth. Mark, my older brother, had a purple tongue for a month." She stopped speaking and wrinkled her nose. "I'm talking too much, aren't I? It's a problem I have. Probably comes from growing up in a large family. If you don't speak up, you don't get heard."

As their dinner was placed in front of them, Ginna dug enthusiastically into her mahi mahi.

"No, I like your candor," he told her. "I have to admit I haven't been out with a woman in a while, but I don't remember enjoying a conversation so much."

"What do you usually talk about with women?"

Whether Emma should take dance classes or tae kwon do with her brother. The subject of my next column on single fathers. Listening to a woman stockbroker tell me what I need in my portfolio.

"Stocks, bonds, whether I have enough life insurance," he admitted. "I know it's not manly—" he twitched his fingers to indicate quotes "—to admit I haven't dated much, but I was never much for intimating I'm a party animal when I'm not."

"No, you're obviously a man secure with yourself. I have a male client who thinks he's Stud of the Year and feels he has to prove it. Luckily for him, he's all talk. He tried propositioning me once. I then explained what my sharp scissors could do to his precious hair. He's behaved since then."

"I would, too." He chuckled. "So tell me what it was like growing up in such a large family."

"Chaotic. Noisy. Wild. My dad restores vintage automobiles. He has his garage on the property. All of us can change our own oil, change a flat tire, even replace all the hoses. Except for my brother Brian. He's a total klutz with a car. Now he uses the excuse that he saves his hands for better things. He's a paramedic, as is my brother Mark. My brother Jeff is a fireman, and my sister, Nikki, is in her junior year of college and talking about going on to medical school. Brian and Jeff are married. Brian has an adorable baby daughter, and Jeff has twin girls and a baby boy."

"I have—" He clamped his mouth shut as Lucie's words slammed their way into his brain. *There's nothing wrong if you take some time away from being Emma and Trey's dad.* He grinned sheepishly. "Twins run in my family. I'm surprised none of your siblings are twins."

"My mother is a twin," Ginna replied. "When we were little, none of us could tell Mom and Aunt Peggy apart. Mom said she was glad none of us were twins. One of each of us was more than enough for her. What about you and your sister?" she asked, turning the tables. "Did you two give your mother any trouble during your rebellious years?"

"Nothing that sent her into hysterics," he admitted. "We're three years apart. At one point in our lives, we seemed a generation apart."

"High school, right?" she asked. "When my brothers were juniors and seniors and I was a freshman, the way they treated me, I might as well have still been in grade school."

"We survived, and some days we figured that was enough," Zach replied.

"That was us. We never allowed anyone to pick on any of us. We did it well enough on our own."

Zach chuckled. "We did that pretty well, too. Still do."

Ginna found herself enjoying both her dinner and the company immensely. They ignored time as they talked their way through dessert. Afterward, Zach suggested a walk along the beach, and she accepted his invitation.

Once they reached the sand, she placed her hand on his shoulder to keep her balance as she slipped off her sandals and he took off his own shoes. She carried them in one hand as they headed across the still-warm sand. A gentle breeze with the tang of salt caressed their faces. Music from the bar drifted toward them.

"It's so beautiful here," Ginna declared, lifting her face to the breeze. "It's as if your body understands the need to slow down and it does exactly that. No rushing around. No feeling the need to be at a certain place at a certain time." She stopped and turned to face the hotel, then faced him as she held out her arms. "Come on, Zach Stone, dance with me."

He laughed uneasily. "Uh, dancing's not exactly my strong suit."

She moved toward him until her breasts lightly touched his chest. She picked up one of his arms and placed his hand on her shoulder. The other hand she took in hers.

"Then we'll just move to the music," she murmured. "You can do that, can't you? You don't think about what you're doing. You just let the music take hold of your soul and your feet will follow."

"All right, but don't blame me if I step on your feet," he warned.

"See, you can do it," she teased a few minutes later.

Ginna hadn't believed in attraction at first sight until now. The minute she met Zach, she felt as if she'd met him before. As if there was some connection....

All points considered, she should be thanking Denny, that lower-than-scum subhuman for cleaning out her account. If he hadn't, she wouldn't have gotten back not only the money he took but damages, which let her take *the* vacation of her life.

Who knows, maybe she'd send him a postcard.

She had no idea how long she and Zach remained on the beach dancing. They didn't stop until the music stopped. Their steps slowed and halted.

She suddenly yawned.

"I'm sorry," she apologized. "I guess everything caught up with me."

"I'll walk you to your room," he offered.

Ginna could feel the sensual pull as they crossed the lobby and entered the elevator.

They didn't speak a word as they reached her floor. Zach walked beside her down the hallway until she stopped at a door.

"Here we are," she said, then silently cursed herself for sounding so inane. She dug her key card out of her bag and inserted it in the slot. When the light turned green, indicating the lock had been released, she reached for the doorknob, but Zach's hand covered it first. He turned it and pushed the door open. She smiled. "Thank you for dinner."

"How about tomorrow?" he asked.

She wanted to say yes so badly she could taste it. At the same time, she was afraid to appear overly eager.

Dating etiquette was so difficult at times!

She decided it was time to throw the rulebook out the window.

"I'll be on the beach in the morning," she said, taking a middle-of-the-road answer.

He smiled back. "Good night, Ginna."

She was aware he waited until she was inside.

"Don't forget the inside bolt." His low voice reached her ears.

She shot it home, hearing a satisfying click. She strained her ears, but there was no chance of her hearing him leave. If it hadn't been the sensation that the air pressure around her fell, she wouldn't have known.

She dropped her sandals into a chair, followed by her purse. She made quick work of undressing and slipping on a cotton nightgown.

It wasn't until the lights were off and she was under the covers that she allowed herself a moment to reflect on her evening.

Her wide smile as she fell asleep was proof enough that her date had been more than a success.

ZACH'S FIRST THOUGHT that something wasn't right was the fact that he woke up on his own. He wasn't grunting as small bodies jumped on top of him with high-pitched demands for breakfast.

He couldn't hear that annoying honking of a car horn out front as the neighbor's teenage daughter's boyfriend liked to do when he picked her up for school.

There were no sounds of *Sesame Street* in the background.

All he could hear was...nothing. Blessed silence.

For a full five minutes, Zach luxuriated in the peace and quiet that he couldn't remember the last time he'd enjoyed. And when the five minutes were up, he felt intense guilt that he felt any joy.

He missed his kids with all his heart and soul, but a part of him admitted this moment of quiet was very nice.

"Not that I'll ever admit it to you, Luce," he muttered as he tossed the covers back and got out of bed. "You'd gloat too much about how right you were in talking me into taking this trip."

A little while later as he ate breakfast in the hotel restaurant, he looked for Ginna. Unfortunately he didn't see the now familiar figure. His food didn't taste as good as it had the previous night, which he put down to the lack of company.

An hour later, as he walked along the beach, he kept a lookout for Ginna but still didn't see her.

"If I didn't know any better, I'd probably start thinking she was nothing more than a dream last night," he muttered, seeing a variety of bikini-clad women but none that resembled one particular woman.

Then he heard a laugh-filled scream from somewhere out in the water.

At first, he thought of all those shark movies, then he realized the owner of the scream was not being attacked by any sea monster, but merely battling the waves and straining to remain upright on a sailboard. She was quickly losing the battle as the sail went one way and she went the other. He waited, watching the spot where she'd fallen. She seemed to pop up out of the water.

"Hi!" she yelled, waving in his direction.

He waited at the water's edge as she swam toward him.

"I just learned sailboards and I aren't a good match," she said, walking up the sand a little ways. She snatched up a towel and rubbed her face, then blotted her hair.

She combed the unruly strands back from her face with her fingers. "Have you ever been on one?"

"Not recently." He couldn't keep his eyes off her. Her bronze-colored one-piece suit covered the essentials and definitely wasn't as revealing as the barely-there bikinis he noticed other women wearing. But it sure caught his attention. Even with wet hair streaming down her back and no makeup, she looked lovely. She also had the grace to make fun of herself.

"Well, that was my last time," she declared. "The next time I might get dumped a lot farther out."

Zach looked down the beach to where a hotel employee oversaw the sailboarders. He was in the midst of instructing a guest.

"Be fun to get out there again," he said. "I haven't done it in years."

"Go for it," she urged. "Show me how it's done." She laid her towel back down on the sand. "I'll even sit here and cheer you on."

"I'm not trying any fancy moves," he warned her. "I'll probably be lucky I don't fall off and break something important."

"Then I'll go with you to the emergency room and mop your fevered brow," she cooed.

Zach grinned. "As good as your offer is, I hope you don't mind if I try to avoid that kind of trip." He left his belongings behind before he headed down the beach.

Ginna noticed she wasn't the only woman watching Zach's progress. He didn't have the chiseled body that comes from long hours at the gym. But his lean athletic build told her he didn't spend all his time in an office, either.

A man wearing a bright-green Speedo walked past her. He slowed and flashed her an inviting grin.

"Oh, hon, I wouldn't if I were you," Ginna said, affecting a sultry Southern drawl. "My husband is the jealous type, and he knows about a thousand different ways to kill someone without leaving a mark on their body."

Unsure whether to believe her or not, the man opted to move off at a faster clip.

She sighed as she picked up her bottle of sunscreen. After applying a coat of lotion, she slipped on her sunglasses and settled back on her elbows with her long legs stretched out in front of her. She looked outward and easily picked Zach out of the surf riders battling the waves.

The attraction between them was already sizzling. She couldn't remember ever experiencing anything this quickly.

She should be scared to death. The attraction between her and Denny had been fast. Something she'd regretted once she'd regained her sanity. They'd gone from a few dates to living together to marrying, and then, after he pretty well told her she was defective, they divorced.

They both wanted kids. Except she couldn't conceive. All she remembered after countless tests was that pregnancy wasn't possible. At first, Denny said it didn't matter. But he'd lied. He wanted a child of his own seed and refused to consider any other options. Since she couldn't give him one, he couldn't forgive her for her imperfections. He married his pregnant lover the day their divorce became final. Ginna wanted to slink off into a corner to lick her wounds, but her family and friends wouldn't allow her to hide. Initially, she hated them for their warfare tactics to get her out of her shell, but later on, she appreciated their concern.

As a result, she hadn't dated much since her divorce.

She preferred keeping herself busy with lots of bookings and spending time with family and friends. What with Brian's wedding and Abby and Jeff having a baby, family parties were plentiful. The salon and day spa had also been busier ever since word got out that their Blind Date Central bulletin board had been successful in matching up the right women with the right men since its conception two years ago.

Who would have thought that a group of women lamenting the lack of available men would turn into Blind Date Central? Blind Date Central was a success from the first day. Women posted pictures of and information about available men they knew but weren't interested in romantically on the board. The women were willing to share, and the men they "sponsored" had an even better chance of meeting the lady of their dreams.

As a result, permanent matches had been made.

She'd helped her sister, Nikki, post their brother Brian's picture on the board, which was promptly snapped up by Gail Roberts, a pediatrician who was now his wife and mother of their baby girl. Another success story.

Ginna had checked out the board a few times but didn't see anyone who rang her chimes, as she liked to say.

If she didn't know any better, she'd think that fate had stepped in and tossed Zach her way.

And she wasn't about to toss him back.

"YOU DID VERY WELL," Ginna told Zach for about the fifth time. "Definitely better than I did. I think the only reason I didn't immediately fall off was I wanted to wait until I was in deeper water so the fall would look more logical."

"Yeah, I did great all right. A ten-year-old kid was telling me what to do," Zach grumbled good-naturedly, wincing as he gingerly lowered his battered body to the sand. "He was out there managing that sail as if he'd been doing it since he was in the cradle."

"It's all that time they spend with their video games. Their hand-eye coordination is miles ahead of ours," she said, even as she asked a waiter to bring them two piña coladas and a bowl of pineapple spears.

Zach grinned sheepishly. "You're doing a good job of soothing my ego."

"Good. And once you have your piña colada, you'll feel even better." She reached for a broad-brimmed hat and plopped it on her head to protect her face. A stripe of aqua-shaded zinc oxide graced the bridge of her nose to save it from burning in the strong sun. "Even better when you dip a pineapple spear in it and then eat it."

"Too bad I didn't hurt anything. Maybe I could have talked you into kissing my booboos."

His provocative comment hung heavily between them.

Ginna sat up on her knees. She leaned forward to whisper, "Then I guess the next time you fall off a sailboard, I'll have to do just that."

He stared into her eyes. "Be careful, sweetheart. I just might hold you to that promise."

Her lips pursed in a kissable pout. "Don't worry, Zach," she murmured, "I always keep my promises."

Zach stood up and started walking back down the beach.

Ginna looked up, startled by his quick retreat.

"Where are you going?" she asked.

"Where do you think I'm going? I'm getting back on that damn sailboard!"

In an instant, her surprised laughter followed him as

he made his way back to the sailboards. One of which, he knew, had his name on it.

Ginna lost track of time as she watched Zach head out to the water. The bright blue-and-white sail was easy for her to track. She picked up a pineapple spear, dunked it in her piña colada the way a doughnut was dunked in coffee. She took a bite of the fruit, enjoying the slight coconut-and-rum taste that had soaked into it. In no time, the pineapple spear was gone and she was munching on a second one.

"If he stays out too long, I'll have to get another bowl of pineapple," she told herself, already eyeing a third spear. "And if he's lucky, I'll save him one."

"YOU'RE A VERY STUBBORN man," Ginna told Zach as they returned to the hotel.

Ginna walked. Zach limped.

"I wasn't going to let a piece of lumber win," he groused.

"And it didn't," she said happily.

"It only took me about three hundred tries to get it right." He straightened up, then groaned. "It was easier when I was younger."

"When you were more agile and flexible?" she said, tongue tucked firmly in cheek. She flashed him a blinding smile when he glared at her. "Younger bodies bounce better. Softer bones," she went on blithely. "At least you landed on water. It's a lot softer than if you landed on, say, cement." She patted his shoulder.

"Small comfort, Ginna," he growled.

"All you need is a good massage and a hot shower, and you'll feel like a new man," she assured him.

He brightened at her suggestion. "Are you going to give me the massage?"

"Not my line of expertise. But I understand the hotel has a lovely spa and a couple of massage therapists. I hear the one named Stan is excellent."

Zach winced and not just because his muscles were protesting every move he made.

"I don't think so," he muttered. "I'll just stick with the hot shower." He stopped at the bank of elevators. "There was a time when I didn't end up looking as if I was ready to fall apart at any second."

Ginna smiled at his confession. "Ah, a man of the millennium." She pushed the call button. "Does this mean you don't want to play tennis this afternoon?" she teased.

"Right now, I wouldn't even play golf if I could swing the club from a golf cart," he told her. He stepped into the elevator after the doors opened. "Still have pity for an old man and have dinner with him?"

"Okay. I'll see you at seven," she said.

He was smiling as the elevator doors closed. A smile that disappeared as soon as the doors slid shut. He leaned against the wall.

"Oh, yeah, you gave the lady a great impression," he muttered. "And on the first day, too. She'll probably wait and call later with an excuse for why she can't meet me tonight, and I can't blame her. I thought chasing after the kids kept me fit. Obviously that fitness routine isn't very reliable."

Zach took his time in the shower, savoring the hot spray as it pounded down on his battered body. By the time he got out and toweled off, he was feeling more like himself but could still feel some stiffness in his arms and legs.

He regretted not bringing his laptop computer along. Writing down his impressions of his vacation could be some good fodder for his column. He pulled stationery out of the desk drawer and began writing. When he got a chance, he'd pick up a notebook in town.

I'm sitting here in paradise. I'll be meeting a beautiful woman for dinner. Is this not every man's dream? After all, the kids are three thousand miles away. So why am I thinking the kids would have a ball here? Yeah, I know I'm a fool.

I'm a single dad who works out of my home. Meeting women isn't easy unless we're parents in the same play group or at the preschool.

But I'm still feeling guilty being here without the kids. Maybe I should look at it another way. Maybe the kids are enjoying a vacation from me. Maybe they're doing all the things I don't allow them to do.

Can any of you tell me why when I woke up this morning, I thought about that beautiful woman instead of my kids? In a sense, I did think about them. I thought about how it felt not having a small body jump on top of me and demand breakfast. I thought about how it felt to hear sounds of the ocean in the background instead of *Sesame Street*.

Then I thought about seeing the lovely lady in a bikini.

You know what this means, don't you? I'll be taking home a small fortune in souvenirs for my kids because I'll feel guilty I didn't take them with me.

And for now, I'm going to enjoy my time with this lady. Do guy-and-girl stuff. I bet there isn't one of you out there who wouldn't do the same thing.

Zach sat back and reread what he'd written. Not bad. Some fine-tuning and he'd have a column in the making, detailing his vacation.

He looked out over the glorious expanse of blue water and white sand.

The man was looking forward to spending time with Ginna. The father was missing his kids big time.

Chapter Three

"Vacation is starting out to be even more than I wished for," Ginna said aloud as she wrote on a postcard she'd already addressed to the salon. "If you only knew." She signed her name and stuck a postage stamp in the corner. "This will make them crazy wondering what's going on." She went on to write short notes on several other postcards to family members. She made sure each note hinted at something good without giving anything away.

She'd hoped to spend most of the day with Zach, but then she thought it over and decided maybe it was better if they didn't spend too much time together. She didn't want him to think she was too eager.

Even if she was feeling pretty impatient to see Zach again.

He might have thought he was less than macho for losing his battle with the sailboard, but she saw it as adorable. A description she knew he probably wouldn't appreciate, but she thought he was pretty special. She'd met more than her share of men who wouldn't have dared admit any type of weakness. It was nice to meet an honest man.

"I'VE COME to the conclusion I wasn't the one having a problem with the sailboard," Zach told Ginna over dinner. They were tucked away in one corner of the hotel's Chinese restaurant. "It was the sailboard. It was definitely possessed by an evil spirit, and I was the idiot who had to battle it."

"So you're thinking if you try a different sailboard, you won't have the problem you had with that one," she guessed.

"I'm not sure it would be a good idea." He moved his rice around on his plate. "Second time around, I might push my luck, get too cocky and really get hurt."

"You're afraid that sailboard will kick your butt," Ginna said bluntly.

Zach winced at her candid, and all too realistic, assumption.

"That, too," he admitted. "Death by sailboard isn't my idea of a suitable epitaph."

She used her chopsticks to corral a piece of ginger chicken. "Don't worry, my brothers wouldn't be able to do it, either. They're happy as clams on a football or baseball field and can do their worst on a basketball court. Anything to do with water is way out of their scope. Even Denny could beat them at water polo," she muttered, choosing a water chestnut next.

"Denny?"

Ginna grimaced. "My ex-husband," she explained. "I usually refer to him as the scum formerly known as Denny. Even if it's because of him I was able to take this trip."

"He wanted you out of the state and sent you here?" Zach asked.

"If he wanted me out of the state, he'd send me to the Amazon jungle, since he knows how much I hate bugs and snakes," she said. "About a month before we got divorced, he cleaned out a bank account that was in my name only. He claimed the money was his. I took him to court. One of my clients works on one of the TV court shows. When she heard I was planning to sue, she suggested I apply to the show. As a result, we ended up on camera. He looked like a total idiot, which wasn't too difficult. The judge saw what an idiot he was, awarded me not only the money he took but punitive damages, since he kept saying he had the right to take the money.'' She looked embarrassed. ''Not one of the finer points in my life. So what about you? Any ex-wives?''

Zach shook his head. ''I was married for six years, but my wife died four years ago,'' he said in a low voice. ''Complications from surgery.''

The way it was explained to him was that she basically bled to death. They couldn't control the hemorrhaging even when they performed a hysterectomy in hopes of stopping the heavy flow. But it was too late. Cathy only saw her babies for a few seconds after they were born. She didn't even have a chance to discuss their ideas for names. In the end he took the names that were at the top of the list. Names written in Cathy's delicate script.

Ginna's expression softened. She reached across the table and covered his hand with hers.

''I am so sorry,'' she said softly. ''I can't imagine what you went through. I bet she was special.''

''She was,'' he said. ''She was an artist. She liked to work in pastels. Chalks. She'd create these incredible landscapes and seascapes that seemed to leap out at you. I wouldn't have thought someone working with chalk could come up with anything so powerful, but she managed to do it.''

"Denny's talent was that he could burp 'Jingle Bells' and crush a beer can against his forehead," she told him. "I'd say you definitely had the better deal. I was really into my stupid period when I met him. He seemed adorable in a Neanderthal way. I was blind to his faults, and by the time I realized what a major mistake I'd made, we were married. Since I was brought up to face my mistakes, I decided to make the best of it. Which didn't work out at all. My parents wanted to throw a party the day I told them I filed for divorce. My dad declared I'd finally come to my senses."

"But it was still hard on you," Zach guessed. "Because you saw it as a failure."

"I wanted a marriage like my parents," she conceded. "But that meant meeting someone who had the same ideals I did. And Denny didn't have them. He wanted things that weren't possible." For a moment pain flashed across her face. "And when he couldn't get them, he blamed me." Her words ended on a bare whisper.

"Because it was easier than blaming himself." Now he was offering the comfort. "We guys are pretty bad about things like that. If he screwed things up between you, it wasn't because of you. It was all him."

"I don't think his new wife would say that." She laughed softly. "But thank you."

"I bet you wished you'd given him a lousy haircut," he said in hopes of lightening the atmosphere.

"I was tempted to offer to give him a haircut, then shave something on the back of his head. 'Kick me' seemed like a good idea."

"Oh, come on, with a little thought you could have come up with something better," he teased.

"Only if I could have insured he'd be arrested the minute he stepped outside." She trapped another piece of chicken with her chopsticks. "Wow, how did we fall into such a heavy subject?"

"It wasn't easy, but we somehow accomplished it."

"You never did say what type of column you write," she pressed. "Do I get a hint?"

"A men's column," he replied.

Ginna nodded. "Sports? Tools? Cars?"

"Single men in today's world." He opted to give her an edited answer.

"Isn't it pretty simple what single guys do in today's world? They hang out in sports bars where they talk about sports, tools and cars," Ginna said. "Not to mention they talk about women, but that's a given."

"Just as women get together and talk about men," he countered.

She inclined her head in silent agreement. "We do have that nasty habit of dissecting the male gender. But you men stand around moaning and groaning all the time that you don't understand us. When all it would take to understand us is to sit there and listen to what we have to say." She stabbed the air with her chopsticks for emphasis.

"But do you always give us the four-one-one we need to understand you?" he argued, using the slang term for information.

Ginna rolled her eyes. "Hello!" she sang out. "Let me give you an excellent example." She closed her eyes in thought, her chin resting in her cupped hand. Her eyes popped open. "Denny's and my sixth-month anniversary. I spent the day at the spa getting gorgeous because we were going to go out for dinner. Wore the slinky dress and everything. Denny comes home from work and asks why I'm so dressed up. Oh, sure, it's our sixth-month anniversary, and yeah, we're going out to dinner. But his idea of dinner was a hot dog at a hockey game.''

''Wow, I'm impressed,'' Zach said with mock reverence. ''Not many guys would consider feeding you first.''

She shot him a fierce glare that experience had taught him only a woman can give.

''What about your sixth-month anniversary?''

Zach got an edgy hunted look.

''I thought we were talking about you,'' he muttered, refusing to meet her eyes.

''And now we're focusing on *you.* So give.'' Her brilliant blue eyes turned steely.

Zach looked away, mumbled something, then quickly returned to his food. He stabbed at a piece of beef with his fork.

''Zach, tell me.''

He mumbled again.

''Excuse me?''

He blew out a breath. ''Fine.'' He snapped off the word like an icicle. ''I bought her a new washer.''

''A washer,'' Ginna repeated. ''As in optional second rinse, dual agitator, heavy-duty-load capacity washer?''

''Yes,'' he grudgingly admitted.

''And I thought my night at the hockey game was bad,'' she mused. ''At least Denny bought me a T-shirt.''

''It was a top-of-the-line washer,'' Zach huffily informed her.

''Which means the salesperson suckered you in to buying more than you needed,'' she translated. ''And what did she say about her oh-so-romantic gift?''

Zach looked as if he wished he was anywhere but there. ''I thought she was hinting for a new washer because she kept talking about my clothes. What she was saying was that if I didn't start picking up my dirty clothing and tossing it in the hamper where it belonged, she'd throw it in a bucket and add bleach. Instead, I lost four perfectly good shirts to a bleach-filled washer.''

''I wish I'd thought of that.'' She pantomimed writing on her hand. ''Definitely something to write down and keep for future reference. You didn't buy a new dryer, too?''

''We got a new one a few months later.'' He looked as if he wanted to chew nails.

''Oh, the nine-month anniversary. Good idea.'' She said it as if it wasn't.

''It was practical.''

''This from the man who writes a column for single men? What do you suggest they give a woman who's going on a first date with them? A pipe wrench?''

''No, actually, I go with the tire-pressure gauge,'' he said, deadpan.

''Zach, Zach, Zach—'' she shook her head ''—I do hair for a lot of single women who are preparing for their first date. Their routine is simple. Hair done in a deceptively casual style that doesn't look styled at all. Hands paraffin-dipped, nails manicured and feet pedicured. Sometimes even a facial and massage. They walk out looking gorgeous. And what happens when their date picks them up? He tells her, hopefully, that she's beautiful and hands her a tire-pressure gauge, instead of flowers? Not a good idea. I can tell you now if a man brought me something like that, he'd be informed just where that tire gauge could go, and I don't mean in a tire, either.'' She waved her hands for emphasis. ''I can see I have my work cut out here.''

''Work?''

"Of course!" She laughed. "On how to be the perfect sensitive man. You forget, I listen to women all day long. And I am a woman. If anyone can set you on the right path, it's me."

The piece of beef Zach tried to swallow seemed to have grown in size.

"Why do I feel as if you're going to throw me into the deep end without a life preserver?"

"You can do it." Ginna patted his hand. She grabbed a morsel of her chicken and held it in front of his lips. "Lesson number one—just nibble," she purred softly.

"Something tells me this lecture series will be the death of me." He obediently followed her instruction.

"Only if you don't listen to the teacher," she cooed, this time taking a piece of chicken for herself. She nibbled on her jasmine rice. "Home appliances are not romantic. You need to be careful with flowers in case the lady in question is allergic. Candy isn't always a good idea because so many women are watching their weight. But one lovely chocolate rose could be a good idea. Or a silk one. Teddy bears are cute, but make sure they're cute-looking teddy bears, not just generic ones."

Zach frowned. "You must date a lot."

Ginna shook her head. "I just do a lot of hair and women talk about dates, where they went and so on. And if it's a bad date, I still get every detail. Sometimes more than I ever wanted to know." She leaned over the table to confide, "One thing to tell your readers? Revealing you're wearing edible underwear is a big no-no."

Zach realized he had in front of him a wealth of information about the opposite sex. And what could turn out to be interesting tidbits for his column. His agent had suggested he do more than write about a single father's life, more about a dad's life beyond the kids.

It didn't hurt that he was strongly attracted to her.

It wasn't difficult when he looked at her with her hair held back from her forehead with a multicolored scarf, the vivid colors of a sunset echoed in the simple sleeveless dress she wore.

"Maybe I should take notes," he commented in a low husky voice that implied he wouldn't mind doing much more than merely taking notes.

"I have an idea you're one of those pupils who learns quickly." She smiled back, as caught up in the flirtation as he was. "This is the first time someone's been interested in anything other than my skill with hair."

"That I can't believe," he argued amiably. "You're breath-stoppingly beautiful."

"Breath-stoppingly beautiful?" She laughed. "You do have a way with words, Zach. I could have used you in middle school when I was taller than most of the boys and skinny as a rail."

"Sorry, at that age I was the typical male teen who didn't look at a girl unless she was amply endowed. Namely, anyone with a D cup."

"Ah, a breast man," she said sagely. "Two of my brothers are breast men, the other strictly a leg man. His fantasy is dating either a hosiery model or a Las Vegas showgirl."

"You can't fault a man for having attainable goals," he pointed out.

She nodded. "True. I thought the basketball-team captain was cute. And he was taller than me, which made it even better."

"But?" He knew there had to be more to the story.

"But—" she drew the word out "—my brothers thought he was a jerk. They told him if he even looked at me, they'd make sure he didn't play basketball again.

I gave two of my brothers a black eye and the other one got ratted out for sneaking out of the house in the middle of the night.''

"So you're one of those who gets even, instead of mad," Zach said.

"You betcha." She picked up her fortune cookie and broke it open. She pulled out the narrow strip of paper and crunched down on her cookie while she scanned the fortune. She tossed the paper onto her plate and reached for Zach's cookie.

"That happens to be my cookie," he said. "My fortune."

"I didn't like mine. Maybe yours is better. But you can have the cookie back." Ginna wrinkled her nose. "Yours isn't much better."

Zach reached across the table and picked up her fortune. "'Your future is like the grains of sand on the desert,'" he read. "This is bad."

"No kidding and yours wasn't much better." She held the paper up. "'Watching the clock will only slow down time even more.' They're almost depressing."

Zach took care of the bill while Ginna excused herself. When she returned, he noticed her lipstick had been reapplied. She slipped her arm through his.

"Another walk on the beach?" he asked.

"I'd love to." Her smile warmed him more than the sun.

As they walked along the beach, they passed other couples out enjoying the evening. The farther they walked, the fewer people they ran across, until they were the only ones.

"Look behind you," Ginna said, spinning around. "It's as if we're suddenly the only people on earth. You can't see the lights from the hotel or even hear the music from the lounge. Our music is the sound of the waves, and the only light comes from the moon." She waved an arm to encompass their surroundings.

"I couldn't be stranded with a better companion. Just think of all the tutoring you could do."

Her hand reached for his and lightly squeezed it. "You'd be a real Romeo by the time I finished."

Zach kept hold of her hand and turned her to face him.

"We're alone now," he murmured, caressing the delicate planes of her face with his fingertips. He lowered his head and easily found her mouth. She moved closer, sliding one hand up his arm until it reached his neck. Her fingers curved around his nape, keeping him there.

Zach had known he was going to kiss Ginna. He'd known that since dinner as he listened to her instruct him in the fine art of being romantic. He'd sat there watching the varied expressions cross her face as she spoke and the animation that lit up her eyes.

He couldn't remember ever before meeting a woman who was so self-assured and comfortable with herself. One of the few times he'd dated, he spent time with a woman who obsessed over every bite of food, worried about drafts when they attended a concert at the Hollywood Bowl. But what killed the date for him was her open disdain for some children who were attending the concert with their parents. When he took her home, she bluntly asked him when they could get together again. That was when he told her he had four-year-old twins. The woman didn't bother saying good-night and he wasn't invited in for a cup of coffee.

He didn't think that would happen with Ginna. She came from a large loving family and had her share of nieces and nephews. And he felt guilty not telling her about the kids right away. He was proud of them. Loved them dearly.

If he thought she was perfect before, kissing her sealed the deal. She was more than he could have imagined.

Her mouth was soft and inviting. Her skin like warm silk under his touch.

He traced the seam of her lips with his tongue, silently asking admission, which was instantly granted. Her tongue wasn't shy as she entered into the play, daring him to follow. A dare he was very happy to accept.

She draped herself around him the way a piece of silk caresses the body. If she was a perfect fit for a kiss, what would she be like if there was more? What if he lay her down on the sand and they—

He stopped his line of thinking.

They may be alone now, but there was no guarantee someone wouldn't come along.

"Lady, you pack quite a wallop," he said once he could catch his breath.

She tipped her head back, eyes closed and lips slightly parted. "Thank you," she said huskily. She swayed in his direction.

Just as he feared, he could hear voices on the wind.

"I think we're going to have company soon." He took several deep breaths, but all he seemed to smell was her perfume. It wasn't helping his peace of mind at all.

Ginna moved to his side and slid her arm around his waist. "Then I guess this would be as good a time as any to go back." Her hip bumped gently against his.

The sexual tension between them heightened with every step. When they were alone in the elevator, Zach took advantage and stole a kiss.

Their steps slowed as they walked down the hallway

to her room. When they reached her door, Ginna turned to face him. He planted his hands on either side of her shoulders, effectively trapping her against the wall. His head dipped and he kissed her again.

"I'm going to be a gentleman and not ask to come in," Zach murmured against her mouth.

Her eyes were hazy with desire. But it was her lips he noticed that were curving upward.

"And what if I invite you in?" she said in a throaty whisper.

He already felt the mental kick to his backside. A kick he'd have physically done to himself if it were possible.

"As much as I'd like to accept, I'd have to be a gentleman and regretfully decline." His mouth slid along the curve of her cheek until it reached her ear. His tongue toyed with her gold hoop earring. "Or at least take a rain check."

"Damn." Her curse came out on a soft breath. "And here I was going to lure you inside and drive you insane with passion."

"I like your plan." He was too engrossed in exploring her ear. He kept his hands planted firmly on either side of her shoulders, because he knew if he touched her elsewhere, he'd never leave. And he should. He wanted to prove to her, and to himself, this was more than just mindless lust. But he knew if he didn't get out of there soon, he'd never leave. "I'm still trying to be a gentleman here. How about tomorrow?"

She pulled back as far as she could, the desire in her eyes starting to dissipate.

"Maybe you're right. Maybe we are going too fast," she said, sensing the truth in his words. "I think it might be better if I did something by myself tomorrow. Then we could get together the next day."

Zach felt the blow. "Twenty-four hours?"

She reached up and kissed him lightly. "More like thirty-six hours. You're proving too addictive, Mr. Stone," she murmured. "I need to catch my breath and I'm already finding out I can't do it when I'm with you. I'll meet you for breakfast the day after tomorrow."

"How about a drink two minutes after midnight? Or if you want to stick with breakfast, we have it at dawn?"

"Dawn? I don't think so. You're not dealing with a morning person here," she explained. "The best I can give you is seven-thirty."

"Seven-thirty, day after tomorrow. If I have to wait that long, I may as well have something that will hold me that long." He pulled her back into his arms, and this time he didn't hold back. He demanded everything of her.

Ginna moaned softly as she melted in his embrace. By the time they parted, they were both breathing heavily.

"Go now." She pushed him away from her.

"A day away from you isn't going to make any difference," he warned her.

"It will if you happen to meet someone else who rings your chimes," she said.

Zach reached out and traced the lush contours of her lips with his fingertip. "You ring my chimes just fine, sweetheart. I'll see you at breakfast, day after tomorrow."

As he walked back to the elevator, he realized that he was already counting down the hours until he saw her again.

It couldn't come soon enough.

Chapter Four

"What in the world can he talk to her about? She has to be all of twelve."

Ginna stretched out on the lounge chair set out on the sand. She had the headphones to her CD player covering her ears, her sunglasses perched on her nose and her hat shading her face. Her skin glistened with sunscreen lotion that smelled strongly of coconut. Since it was only late morning, the colada she held was a virgin.

At the moment, her drink was forgotten as she covertly watched Zach and a young woman standing down by the hut where sailboards were signed out by the guests. Her dark glasses hid her narrowed gaze.

"Honestly, Zach, I thought you had more sense than to fall for a pair of perky breasts," she muttered. "Can you spell much too young? But then, how could your brain work when you're facing a girl wearing nothing more than a few strands of colored dental floss? I'm sure she's illegal in more than one state."

The focus of Ginna's attention was the kind of sexy young woman that caused any red-blooded man to salivate. Petite with curves in all the places, she wore a bright red thong bikini that left very little to the imagination. Glossy black curly hair tumbled down around her deeply tanned shoulders. She looked up at Zach as if he was he was the answer to all her prayers.

Ginna had no idea what Zach said, but apparently the young woman found it humorous, because she laughed and tossed her hair back. And managed to lift her chest at the same time.

Ginna curled her lip.

"I didn't mean it when I said you might find someone who rang your chimes," she ground out, slurping up the rest of her drink. She considered flagging down a waitress and asking for a non-virgin piña colada. "But if you had to find someone, couldn't you find someone who doesn't have a curfew?"

"Is anyone using this lounger?" A male voice sounded from her left.

She turned her head and looked up. And up.

Tall. Very tall. Maybe six foot, five inches. Surfer-blond hair. Blue eyes that rivaled her own. A tanned body that could easily grace the cover of a fitness magazine.

Any other woman would have melted into a puddle by now. By all rights, Ginna should be drooling uncontrollably, suffering heart palpitations and possibly stammering while making sure to show her bikini-clad body to its full potential.

Ginna wasn't drooling, her heart rate was perfectly steady, and her speech, when she answered the man, was coherent.

In fact, she didn't feel anything at all.

She could have been looking at one of her brothers.

WHO THE HELL IS HE? And what makes him think he can move in on Ginna that way? Zach might have looked as if he was listening to barely clad Kendall, but he was really focusing on Ginna.

He knew to the second the moment she took possession of the beach lounger, laying her towel over the surface, then settling down on it. He thought he'd die when she applied lotion to her exposed skin. Once finished, she popped a CD into her portable player and settled the headphones in place. He knew to the second when she ordered a drink. And damn, some surfer dude was trying to put the moves on her. Even from this distance, Zach felt blinded by the guy's pearly whites.

He'd come down here with the intention of wearing himself out on a sailboard. What he hadn't expected was sweet *young* Kendall Taylor to latch on to him.

"So how long are you staying here, Zach?" She looked up from under the cover of lush dark eyelashes.

"A couple weeks," he replied in a voice meant to deter, but all it seemed to do was entice her.

"Really? So am I," she purred.

Zach had never felt more of an urge to scream for help. This woman was way too dangerous for him.

Kendall wasn't old or experienced enough to let her natural sensuality speak for itself. She tried too hard to behave in a sexy fashion, which turned him off, thank God. But he hazarded there were at least twenty men there who'd be willing to take what she was offering. He wasn't one of them.

He snuck a quick glance in Ginna's direction again. Mr. Blond and Beautiful took the lounger next to her. His gestures and grins were meant to look boyish and appealing. Zach figured them to be as fake as his gleaming teeth.

If she was crazy enough to fall for the toothpaste poster boy, he wouldn't have much respect for her.

Dammit, she was smiling at the guy! That smile that instantly aroused Zach.

What could she be smiling about?

"Perhaps we could get together later for a drink," Kendall murmured, moving in closer until the clean sea air seemed tainted by her musky perfume.

Zach felt as if a noose was slowly tightening around his neck.

Damn, he was glad he'd met Ginna. No matter what, he wouldn't have succumbed to Kendall's oh-so-obvious charms. He looked down at red-glossed pouty lips.

"Kendall, what are you—seventeen, eighteen?"

She straightened. "I am twenty," she said haughtily.

He doubted her twentieth birthday was in the near future.

"Oh, honey, I have T-shirts older than you," he said gently. "You should be off chasing some guy closer to your own age." *Like that surfer hitting on Ginna.*

Kendall's smile turned to pure sex kitten. "They're nothing more than boys eager to show off their muscles." She rested her hand on his arm. "I happen to like older men. They know how to treat a woman."

Zach silently vowed to never again talk to any female between the ages of twelve and thirty.

"Yeah, but we also break down a lot sooner."

Kendall studied his face. Her resigned expression told him she finally realized she wasn't going to get anywhere with him.

"You'll regret it, you know." She propped one hand on her hip.

"I don't think so." He delivered the blow as softly as he could.

"Well, if you change your mind, I'll be around." She flashed him another sex-kitten smile and walked off with hips swiveling in a way guaranteed to catch any man's attention.

Zach noticed she did just that. He had the urge to wrap a towel around her barely clad derriere.

At the same time a frightening thought hit him like a thunderbolt.

His encounter with the young woman gave him a glimpse of his future as the father of a teenager. In about thirteen years Emma would be the same age as Kendall, and he would have to play the heavy, scaring off hormone-driven teenage boys. He feared he'd not survive Emma's teenage years.

For now, he was going to take a sailboard out into the water and conquer the damn thing even if it killed him.

"WHAT DOES IT TAKE for someone to understand the word no?" Ginna grumbled as she marched down the hallway leading to the rest room. The only place she was certain he wouldn't follow her into. "It comprises two letters, one syllable, and the idiot doesn't get it. I swear whatever bleach he's using on his hair has seeped into his brain."

She'd spent the past hour convincing Tad that no, she wouldn't meet him for drinks. Or have dinner with him. And a big no to going out on a boat with him at midnight to watch the stars. It was as if with each refusal, he grew more determined to tempt her into the perfect date.

He saw himself as the perfect catch for a woman.

She saw him as a man with an ego much larger than his brain.

She was about to push open the door to the ladies' room when someone grabbed her hand and spun her around, setting her back against the wall. She was ready to fight back when she realized just who had hold of her.

"Did you ever think about saying a person's name so you wouldn't scare the hell out of them?" she gasped, pushing Zach away from her. He obligingly stepped back. He was still wet from his time in the water.

"You were too busy mumbling. Sounded like a curse on the male sex. What happened? Did Junior say a bad word?"

"The curse only involves one member." She took a deep breath. "What happened to Miss Perky? Did her baby-sitter show up?"

Zach blinked. He laughed softly and shook his head as he recognized her tone.

"Perky?"

"Perky as in she's not old enough to worry about gravity taking over," Ginna said with a decided bite in her voice.

"You mean like the surfer hanging all over you?" Zach countered.

"Tad is an interesting conversationalist," she lied.

"Tad?" he echoed. "You're kidding, right?"

"I would never kid about a name like that." Ginna glared at him.

"Maybe we should introduce him to Kendall."

"Kendall? And you made fun of Tad's name?" She suddenly remembered their pact. "You have another fourteen hours, mister."

"Too bad. No more of this seeing if there's someone else who might ring my chimes," he ordered.

Ginna arched an eyebrow in disbelief. "I don't know, it seemed your little friend Kendall rang an entire chorus."

Zach muttered a few swear words he'd never dare use around the twins.

"Look," he ground out, "you thought we were taking

it too fast. Fine, we'll slow things down. I have no desire to go running after anything with breasts. I don't know what's going on between us, but I want the chance to find out. And I think you want the same thing. Unless Tad rang your chimes?'' he challenged.

She blew out a breath of exasperation. ''Oh, please. He was relentless in his hopes I'd go out with him. It got so bad I finally told him I was a lesbian to make him give up,'' she said bluntly.

The corners of Zach's mouth tipped upward. ''What did he say?''

Ginna rolled her eyes. ''He's positive he's the man who can convert me.''

He leaned in further. ''Is he?'' His breath was warm on her face.

''Well—'' she drew out the word ''—I always was a sucker for blonds.''

He moved in even closer until his chest brushed the tips of her breasts. Her nipples tightened in response.

''There is something to say about a man with experience,'' she murmured. Her eyes gleamed like blue topaz gems. ''The self-confidence that comes with it.'' Her soft laughter was smothered by his mouth.

Instant heat flared between them as their mouths fused. Nothing mattered but the touch.

When they paused for breath, Ginna stared blankly at her surroundings. She was amazed no one had come upon them. But then, an entire marching band could have gone past them and she wouldn't have been aware of it.

''You are a dangerous man,'' she said when she felt she could speak coherently.

''Must have something to do with the company I

keep. So are we in accord? I'll keep Little Boy Blond away from you.''

She smiled. ''Tad's pre-law.''

''They teach that in preschool now?''

''Be careful, Zach, or I won't run interference with your junior miss,'' she said, smiling.

He dipped his head and ran the tip of his tongue along her bottom lip.

''She's twenty.''

''She's sixteen if a day.''

''Then Kendall and Tad will make the perfect couple.''

Ginna pushed him back again before she did something totally insane. Such as drag him up to her room and have her way with him.

''I have to go. I have an appointment in an hour,'' she told him.

He arched an eyebrow in silent question.

''For a massage and a few other pick-me-ups,'' she clarified.

''Dinner tonight?''

''So much for our pact.'' She gave a sigh. ''I can't be ready until around eight.''

''Eight o'clock. In the lobby.''

Ginna nodded and left quickly, while Zach strolled away in the other direction. Both had broad smiles on their faces.

GINNA KNEW she'd truly come to paradise. It had been several days since she and Zach decided time apart didn't work for them. She'd met Zach that night after a relaxing session in the hotel's spa. Just as before, they talked nonstop during dinner, then spent a few hours in the lounge, talking and dancing.

She didn't want to think of their time together as having a time limit. The idea that their feelings for each other could change when they returned home was a thought she kept tucked away in a secure place where it couldn't easily creep out and haunt her when she least expected it.

She and Zach had smiled when they first noticed the seductive and relentless Kendall advance on Tad with the kind of focus the military would envy. The young couple had been inseparable ever since.

Ginna should have been in heaven. So why did she feel as if she was teetering on the brink of hell? She knew a good part of it was due to the sexual tension between her and Zach, which had gotten so taut she was surprised glass didn't shatter when they walked past windows and mirrors.

She knew he wanted her. So why didn't he do something about it? Each night when they parted with kisses, their parting took longer. It had been touch and go on her part, pardon the pun. It was taking more and more restraint to not grab hold of his shirt and drag him into her room.

She told herself that they were making a point. That what was happening between them was about more than sex. So far, they hadn't run out of things to say. They constantly touched each other as if needing that reassurance.

By all rights, she should be scared to death. She'd joked to her friends that she'd have a vacation romance, but she wasn't looking for anything more.

Except when she'd said that, she hadn't met Zach.

They'd decided to get away from the hotel today. Zach left after breakfast to rent a car. Ginna was able to get a cooler from the hotel, and she filled it with bottled water and snacks. Their plan was to drive up to the rim of an ancient volcano and a series of springs that flowed into a waterfall leading to the ocean.

Dressed in a tropical-print miniskirt and blue sleeveless cowl-neck knit top, she chose sneakers for ease in walking over the uneven terrain they would be encountering during their trek. Armed with sunglasses, a camera and a couple of beach towels, she stood outside the hotel waiting for Zach to show up.

When he pulled up in front of her, she stared at his mode of transportation.

"This is a Jeep." She didn't move.

"Yep." He hopped out. "The agent said it was better for what we have in mind."

"Better for what? Crossing the Sahara? Climbing the Rockies? I thought we were just driving up to see a volcano and some special pools of water." She gave the vehicle a dubious look.

"We are. The road we'll be traveling on winds all the way up. You don't get carsick, do you?" Zach picked up the cooler and tossed it into the rear.

"No." Ginna still hung back. "Look," she appealed to him with hands outstretched. "Not that I'm a killjoy or anything and I'm definitely not a snob. But Jeeps, especially older ones, seem…well…"

"Rustic?" he supplied.

"Bone-jarring."

Zach practically pushed her up into the vehicle. "You'll be fine." He ran around and hopped in behind the wheel.

She grabbed hold of the dashboard as he drove off. "Is there something we don't know about this road?" she shouted.

"It's paved!" he shouted back. "What more do you need to know?"

Ginna thought of many things she wanted to know. The first came to mind the moment they turned off the highway onto the marked road going up the side of the volcano.

She leaned over and yelled in his ear, "You could have asked just what century this road was paved!"

"Where's your sense of adventure?" His face was aglow with excitement.

Ginna whimpered. "Back at the hotel," she muttered, hanging on to the seat as she bounced up and down, courtesy of the uneven road. "They said this set of pools is a popular tourist spot, right? Are you sure we took the right road?"

He pointed to a sign by a small tower of rocks. "It's clearly marked."

"It should say, 'Enter at your own risk,'" she shrieked when one pothole sent her bouncing upward so hard the top of her head hit the tarp overhead. She sent a prayer of thanks that she wasn't riding in a hardtop car. And a curse that she'd chosen this skirt, instead of shorts today. With the bumpy road, the hem was moving up rapidly to become a waistband. She was fighting a losing battle to keep herself proper.

"Look over there." Zach pointed a second before he pulled off the road and stopped the Jeep. Although the engine had stopped rumbling, her body hadn't.

"It's a waterfall," Ginna said. "Possibly the fifth or sixth we've seen since we turned onto this road."

Zach climbed out and walked around the hood. "Look at the arrangement of lava rocks around it," he said in a voice that bordered on awe.

"They all have lava rocks around them." She hopped

out, then grabbed hold of the door when her knees started to buckle.

He grabbed her arm and held her upright until her equilibrium returned.

"No, this is different." He walked back to the rear of the Jeep and rummaged for the camera. "Come on. Stand in front of it."

"Didn't we do this at the last waterfall?" she mumbled, moving over to stand in front of the flowing water.

Ginna never considered herself a grumpy person. Sure, she had her moments. Who didn't?

"Zach, I feel as if I've spent the last hour inside a blender."

She shouldn't complain. She'd wanted to make this trip as much as Zach did. She just hadn't expected it to be bordering on primitive. She allowed herself to be guided to just the right spot, widened her lips in a smile while Zach snapped away.

"We're almost there," he assured her, dropping his arm around her shoulder as they walked back to the Jeep.

Before she climbed in, she opened the cooler and pulled out two bottles of water. She offered one to Zach. He emptied half the bottle in what looked like one swallow as he studied the map the rental agent had provided.

"Should only be a few miles more," he promised.

"The brochure said a scenic drive up a volcano to sacred pools of water." She bit off each word. "I didn't realize the road would be so rough."

He kissed her on the forehead. "You'll love it."

"All right, I promise not to be so cranky." She walked around and climbed back into the Jeep.

"Wait until you see the pools. The rental agent said they're fantastic. And they're deep enough to swim in."

"Swimming I can do."

The few miles turned into a forty-minute bone-jarring drive. Zach parked along the side of the road near a couple of cars.

"We walk from here," Zach told her as he hopped out. He pulled a backpack out and filled it with necessities.

She picked up her straw hat and plopped it on top of her head. "Lead on, Bwana."

They walked side by side along a dirt path smoothed by the tread of many feet.

She grinned as she listened to Zach's enthusiastic ramblings about their surroundings.

How could she be cranky around him? They were spending time together. She enjoyed being with him. It wasn't as if she was bored with him. The last word she'd use to describe Zach was boring.

She watched him walk in front of her. The khaki shorts he wore were faded and clung lovingly to a nicely defined set of buns. His blue polo shirt was so faded it was a bare whisper of color.

He's probably had it since high school. He looks like one of those dads you see on weekends with their kids.

"I'm surprised since you were married for a while that you didn't have children," she said suddenly.

Zach stumbled. He swore under his breath and spun around.

"Why did you say that?"

She shrugged. "I don't know. I looked at your shirt and for some reason thought of these dads I see on the weekends with their kids. You were married for a few years, and for some reason, I wondered why you didn't have children."

"I could ask you the same. Why you and what's his name didn't have kids."

"Denny? Please. He was as bad as a two-year-old. My nieces and nephews are enough. My brothers are giving my parents plenty of grandchildren without me having to add to the zoo."

Zach grew very still for a moment, then turned back around. "There's the springs."

Ginna walked faster until she stood beside him. She looked down the small hill to a series of four pools of water that ran from one to another, with the last ending in a waterfall that dropped into the ocean. No one else was nearby, which made Ginna feel as though she and Zach were the only ones on the island.

She sighed at how beautiful it was. All the bruises she knew she'd received from the bumpy ride were worth it after seeing this view.

"Ginna?"

She turned to Zach.

"What is wrong?" he asked.

She had two choices.

She could spin more than a few lies that would make him feel better and make her feel worse because she'd lied.

Or she could tell him the truth, which would either have him running away from her, or to her.

"Fine, you want to know what my problem is?" she asked. "*You* are my problem." She held up her hand to indicate he not say one word. "Give me one good reason why you haven't tried to make love with me." Now that she'd started, she found it difficult to stop. "I know for a fact you're interested. I can *feel* it. So what the hell is the problem?"

WHOA, WHEN THE LADY makes a stand, she does it with a capital S.

Zach stood there staring at her. She stood with her eyes flashing blue laser blasts at him and the fury emanating from her body until it fairly quivered with temper.

Damn, she was beautiful.

"Is this one of those times when I flunked the romantic part?" he asked.

She just glared at him.

He tried again. "I'm trying to act like a gentleman?"

She wasn't buying that story, either. Should he tell her the truth? That he'd gone to bed every night hurting because he wanted her so badly.

"I wanted to know that what we have is more than sexual attraction."

That didn't fly, either.

He was starting to lose his temper, too.

"Dammit, Ginna! You think it's been easy for me? I've been going to bed every night aroused because—"

"You respected me?" she sniped.

"Because I want more from you than a roll in the hay!" He shouted so loud even the seagulls gave him a wide berth.

"Fine, we've proved we can talk to each other but—" she paused to take a breath "—I don't want to say goodnight to you anymore and watch you leave."

Zach spun around, running his hand through his hair.

"Damn, Ginna, you've got great timing, you know that? We're miles from the hotel. And I don't think you'd be happy with finding some privacy behind a bush."

She asked you why you didn't have children. A perfect chance for you to tell her. "Didn't I tell you? I have two kids. A boy and a girl. Twins. Four years old."

And then she'd wonder why he hadn't told her before.

You really are out of practice with this stuff.

He shook his head to clear it. Then took a step toward her. And another. And another, until his nose was practically against hers.

"We are going down there and admiring the pools up close," he murmured. "Then we'll climb partway up the volcano. We'll discuss this further after dinner, if that's all right with you?"

She didn't blink or look away. "Fine."

If there had been a bush within dragging distance, they would have been behind it by now.

Zach never thought of himself as some kind of primitive man who took his woman whenever he felt like it.

His woman.

He didn't look away as long as she kept her eyes on him.

She purposely moved forward so that her breasts brushed against his chest. He felt an instant arousal.

"After dinner," he murmured.

"Of course," she murmured back.

Ginna walked ahead of him, her hips swaying as she moved.

Zach was positive she did everything to drive him crazy. She slipped off her sneakers and walked carefully into the water. She exclaimed the water was warm and invited him to join her. She splashed water in his direction.

"Come on, Zach," she shouted, splashing more water at him.

He sat down on the ground and slipped off his backpack and shoes.

"You better be prepared to get good and wet," he threatened.

Ginna shrieked and tried to escape the waves he

splashed her way. Except she turned too fast, slipped on a rock and fell on her butt before he could grab her.

Ginna sat there for a moment, stunned by what had just happened. Then she burst out laughing.

Her laughter seemed to make the tension between them disappear.

"So all it took was a good soaking?" Zach teased.

She looked up. "What?"

He held out his hand. "If I'd known all you needed was a good dunking—" was all he got out before she took his hand and pulled hard.

Zach didn't have a chance. He started to pitch forward and immediately reared back in hopes of keeping his balance, but all it meant was that he also fell on his butt. Water splashed up around him.

Ginna howled with laughter.

"The dunking helping you any?" she asked between giggles.

"Oh, yeah, I feel great." He leaned forward, resting his arms on his knees. "Almost as good as a cold shower." He kept her gaze prisoner. "Almost."

The last thing he expected to see was a wave of color travel up her throat.

He got to his feet and held out his hand again. This time, she curled her fingers around his and allowed him to pull her upward.

"Good thing I'm wash-and-wear," she joked, ineffectively smoothing her skirt down her thighs as they waded back to the water's edge.

"Cute touch, Gin," he murmured from behind.

"What?"

"Your underwear matching your top."

Ginna started to pitch forward and would have landed in the water face first if Zach hadn't grabbed her in time.

Chapter Five

She'd done it. She'd come right out and asked the question. Come to think of it, she'd almost screamed the question at him.

And after hearing it, Zach hadn't run from her or thought she was crazy.

She'd gotten the question out without sounding too much like an idiot. It had come to the point where she was beginning to question her sexual appeal.

The climb up the volcano wasn't easy. She only kept on going by reminding herself that what she was doing was good for her legs. Once they reached the top, she dropped onto a boulder to catch her breath.

"This is nothing like step aerobics," she wheezed.

"You need to do more hiking," he told her, pulling a water bottle out of his backpack and handing it to her. "Use the cross trainer during your workouts."

She thanked him and gulped it down. "The thing that makes you feel like you're walking on water?"

"If you used it thinking you'd be able to walk on water, you sure flunked down there." Zach inclined his head toward the pools.

"Now you know why I don't use it." She handed him back the bottle.

"Don't worry, going back will be easier."

Ginna stood up and looked down into the crater. "Hard to believe there was a time when this exploded in ash and lava," she murmured. "That everything around here died in seconds."

"But beauty came from it, too." He crouched down, studying a tiny white flower. "Look at this. So delicate and yet hardy at the same time."

She hunched down beside him. She turned her head and smiled. "You really are a softie."

He smiled back. "A romantic?"

"Oh, yeah."

Zach straightened and helped her to her feet. He kept his hand clasped warmly with hers.

"Lord, you are beautiful," he said with quiet awe.

"Even when I'm still damp and have straggly hair?" She pulled at her snarled curls.

He brushed his lips across hers. "You think you're damp now?" he murmured against her lips. "Wait until later."

Ginna was positive her heart didn't start beating again until they were back in the Jeep.

What does one wear to a seduction?

Do we use my room or his?

The few times Ginna had been with a man, it was easy. They'd go back to her house and he'd spend the night.

Except now her house was more than three thousand miles away.

What to wear was pretty easy.

The tangerine silk dress was so form fitting she wondered if she'd be able to breathe in it. A birthday gift last year from her sister-in-law Abby. Ginna loved the dress but wondered if she'd ever have the nerve to wear it.

She'd tossed it in her suitcase because she thought she just might get wild enough to wear it. It was time to get wild.

She hadn't taken this much time with her appearance for quite a while. When she finished, she stepped back and studied her reflection in the mirror.

Her hair was swept up in a careful mass of curls that looked casual. The tangerine dress hugged every curve and looked positively illegal. Luckily she had perfume to go with the dress. Her makeup was shadings of bronze, shimmery taupe and cream, which made her eyes look even bluer. She carefully applied bronze lipstick.

"Oh, yes, the lady is ready to be seduced," she murmured.

She picked up her small evening bag and headed for the door. Zach was already downstairs when she stepped off the elevator.

As though sensing her arrival, he turned around. She was still far enough away that she couldn't hear the words he was speaking, but deep down inside she knew they were meant for her. He was looking away, and turned when he realized she was there.

The light in his eyes told her all she needed to know.

She took two steps in his direction.

He took three. He grasped her hands in his.

"If we didn't have an audience right now…" he murmured.

She tipped her head to one side. "Yes?"

"Dammit, Ginna, you knew exactly what you were doing by wearing that dress," he breathed. "Every man here is looking at you."

She smiled at him. "I wouldn't know. I'm only look-ing at you."

Zach's eyes blazed a white-hot fire. "I definitely need a cold drink."

When they entered the bar, Ginna noticed a few women looking in Zach's direction. She made sure her hand on his arm let them know the man was taken.

She needn't have worried. His eyes were only on her.

They ordered drinks. She was barely aware of the taste of coconut and juices on her tongue, along with a bite of alcohol. A platter of appetizers had been set on their table. She picked up teriyaki chicken on a small skewer. She bit one piece off, then offered the rest to Zach. He leaned over and bit off a piece.

"Did I tell you I love that dress?"

She shook her head.

"Then I guess I didn't tell you that I'd also like to see that dress off you."

Ginna smiled. "Then I guess we're even. While I think you look very handsome tonight, I wouldn't mind seeing your clothes off, either."

This time she clearly heard his soft-spoken curse. She dipped her forefinger in her drink and stirred the liquid.

"Did you know that anticipation is the greatest aph-rodisiac?" she asked, slowly licking the drink off her finger.

Zach couldn't take his eyes off her actions.

"Enough," he said through gritted teeth.

He didn't waste any time summoning the waitress for the check. Ginna smiled as she noticed he gave the young woman a very generous tip.

She sensed it was a good thing they were alone in the elevator. The air fairly shimmered with sexual tension.

He walked closely behind her as they moved down

the hallway to her room. The light glowed green as she inserted her key card. She pushed it open and walked inside the room.

A lamp burning in a corner of the room was their only light as she turned around to face him.

Zach stepped into the room.

Ginna kept her eyes on him as she took a step back.

He kicked the door shut behind him.

She stepped forward.

He met her more than halfway.

Her arms encircled his neck at the same time his circled her waist and pulled her against him.

His hunger for her was voracious as he feasted on her mouth. Her dress was unzipped and dropped to the carpet.

He leaned back just enough to look at her.

"You're trying to kill me, aren't you," he breathed as he reached for the clip holding up her hair. He tossed it to one side and ran his fingers through the silky strands. "You had to know what that dress would do to me. What *you* do to me."

"I'm getting a good idea." She nimbly unbuttoned his shirt and pulled the tails out of his waistband. She pushed it off to fall near her dress. "And you're still overdressed." She worked on his belt, as eager as he was.

Zach looked at Ginna, sexy as hell in a pair of cream-colored bikini underwear and high heels that made her legs go on forever. With her hair wild about her shoulders, she looked like someone out of any red-blooded man's dream. He fumbled with the button at his waistband while she took care of the zipper. He'd never been stripped so quickly.

It was suddenly too far to the bed, but they somehow

managed to make it there. Zach fell back on the bed with Ginna falling on top of him.

"You're not going to mind if we don't have dinner first?" he asked. "Or our talk?"

"Does it look like I'm complaining?" She laughed against his mouth. "Oh, Zach, shut up and kiss me."

Kissing her was the easy part. Discovering that she still had on those sexy shoes as she straddled his hips sent his blood pressure soaring, along with other parts of his body as her bare breasts brushed his chest. He raised his head just enough to fasten his mouth on a nipple. She closed her eyes in sheer bliss and moaned deep in her throat as he drew it into his mouth.

"Ambrosia," he murmured.

"Just don't stop," she commanded.

"I don't intend to."

He'd thought her skin was silky before, but now he felt as if she flowed over him. She tasted like nothing on earth. He ran his hands down her back, feeling the delicate curve of her spine that led down to a rear end rounded just right for a man's hands. *His* hands. He tried to roll her over, but she was having none of it.

"Sorry, handsome, you're on my turf now," she said throatily. "My room. My rules."

"As long as this ends up with both of us naked, I'm in your hands." He choked when he realized he literally *was* in her hands.

"You were saying?" she murmured.

"You got my attention," he groaned as he felt her cool touch against his ultrasensitive skin.

"That's not all I've got," she whispered in his ear just before the tip of her tongue traced the shell. "Why, Mr. Stone, what large—" She almost swallowed her words when she realized he was returning the favor. She arched up as he gently probed her with his fingers. "Fast learner." She gasped.

Obviously he'd found just the right spot. He gently pressed again, feeling her muscles tighten around him. He hungered for the moment he would feel her tighten around another part of him, a part that was straining for her.

"It has something to do with those 'come and get me' shoes of yours," he said hoarsely, nibbling his way up her throat. She made it easier for him as she tipped back her head for easier access.

"Talk is cheap, Zach. Show me." Ginna cradled him in her hands.

"Anything for the lady." He proceeded to make good on his promise as he rolled them over until he now lay on top of her. Then he slid her panties down her legs.

Her taut belly quivered under the taunting licks of his tongue. When he reached the source of her heat, she couldn't stop saying his name. Something he didn't mind hearing as he continued to find ways to drive her even higher. He remained in tune with her, sensing when she was ready to explode, then he would back off, blowing soft breaths across skin that responded with shivers. Each time he pushed her senses just a bit more until she was raining a variety of curses on his head.

"Sadist!" She sobbed, even as her legs lifted to hook at the small of his back.

"It will get better," he promised.

"Better?" she almost shrieked as he started it again, but this time when she began that otherworldly climb, he moved upward and thrust into her.

She shattered just as he buried himself deeply inside her.

He'd never imagined anything like this. She closed

tightly around him, her innermost muscles squeezing him until he thought his head would burst.

At the same time, he withdrew and thrust again. And again. Ginna's nails dug into his back, and he concentrated on not losing control.

Ginna kept saying his name over and over as she raised her head to press her mouth to his.

The sight of her face, tight with the same desire that captured him, was enough to keep him going until she exploded again. This time, he burst into flames with her.

If he died now, he knew he'd die a happy man.

"My, my, Mr. Stone, you certainly know how to greet a girl," Ginna said, still breathless from their activity.

He lifted a hand that felt about three hundred pounds heavier than it had before. It flopped back down. That was when he realized that the bedcovers were more off the bed than on and they were lying diagonally across the mattress. He considered them lucky they hadn't rolled off completely.

"I'm not sure, but I think I left my body at some point," he said once he was able to form the words. "For all I know, it hasn't returned yet."

She rolled over and dropped a kiss on his chest.

"Now I understand what they mean by the word *ravished*." She brushed a kiss across his mouth before she nestled her head on his chest. "Doesn't that word sound so earthy? Ravished," she repeated, then released a deep sigh. "Why did we wait so long?"

"I was being a gentleman, remember?"

She idly ran a hand over his chest, tangling her fingers in the crisp curling hairs.

He couldn't believe that she could stir him again so quickly. He thought he'd been drained dry. Not to mention he didn't feel as if he could move a muscle. Obviously parts south had incredible recuperative powers.

"Tell me something, handsome." She flashed a siren's smile at him. "Have you ever been ravished?"

"I thought I just was," he said, his breathing quickening.

Damn, even after everything, she still had those sexy shoes on.

"Oh, no," Ginna murmured, lifting herself and sliding over him. "That was just the appetizer. Now it's time to move on to the main course."

"NOTHING BUT THOSE SHOES," Zach said lazily. "My kind of woman."

Ginna's smile was feline content. She lifted a leg. "Like them, do you?" she purred.

"Hell, I'm ready to glue them to your feet." He kept his eyes fastened on her feet.

She laughed softly. "Careful. People will think you have a shoe fetish."

"With you I could easily develop one."

Ginna stretched her arms over her head. She noticed that Zach's gaze shifted to her breasts. They'd made love twice and she was still hungry for him.

She'd never felt comfortable lying naked with a man. During sex was all right, but just lying there afterward always made her want to cover up.

Not so with Zach. She liked lying there knowing he watched her. Desired her.

Just as she liked looking at him. He was beautiful, but she doubted he'd appreciate being called that. Even his feet were beautiful.

Hm, that saying about big feet...

She smiled because she couldn't stop smiling. She felt way too good.

The phrase "well and truly loved" came to mind. Probably something she'd read in a book. Something else she now understood.

Except now another kind of hunger was starting to make itself known.

"Zach," she purred, "this hotel has a wonderful concept."

"What?" He looked the way she felt.

"Room service." She pursed her lips as she formed the words. "If I make a call, they'll actually deliver food to the room. Besides—" she looked mournfully at her dress lying on the carpet "—I don't think my dress survived."

He sent the dress a fond look. "I'm not too sure I'd want anyone else to see you in it. Especially if you're also wearing those shoes. Most men couldn't handle the shock."

Her smile widened. "Oh, but you can."

"A tough job, but someone's got to do it," he told her.

She slid off the bed and walked to the desk. She pulled out the room-service menu. "Anything you'd like in particular?"

The wicked gleam in his eye gave her his answer.

"For food," she stressed the words. "Sustenance. Fuel for our bodies."

"Red meat," he said promptly, baring his teeth at her.

She shook her head in mock disgust, clucking her tongue. "I swear the male ego gets bigger all the time."

"Thank you."

Ginna's glare held no heat as she picked up the phone and tapped out the number for room service.

"One very large steak, raw, for the barbarian on my bed," she muttered amidst Zach's laughter.

"NOW THAT you've had your way with me, I suppose you'll suddenly find yourself too busy to bother with me," Zach said, waving his fork at her. She leaned over and stole the piece of steak stuck on the tines. "I can see it now. You won't return my calls. I'll just be a discarded plaything in your eyes."

He'd pulled on his pants before room service showed up, but had remained shirtless and shoeless. Ginna put on her robe, a sensual slither of copper-colored satin that clung lovingly to her body.

Ginna widened her eyes with mock innocence. "And here I thought I'd hidden that side of myself so well. What can I say?" She lifted her chin in a haughty manner. "I love 'em and leave 'em." She leaned over to steal another bite of steak, but he pulled his fork back in time to pop it in his mouth. She shrugged an "oh, well" and returned to her salad. "It's not as if this was your first time," she said flippantly.

Zach affected a deep sigh. "How little you know. Just plunder my treasures and then toss me aside."

Ginna was sipping her wine when he spoke. She started choking and had to endure his helpful slap on the back that almost pushed her over the table.

"You are a very bad man," she said, enunciating each word.

"That's not what you said an hour ago."

"There are times when bad is very good. And you are very bad," Ginna purred, aware she meant the exact opposite. The flare of Zach's nostrils told her he knew exactly what she meant. She was relentless. "Very, very bad." She pursed her lips in a seductive pout.

''Now you've done it. Next time, I get to blow your mind.''

She smiled. ''I'm looking forward to it.''

SEX SHOULD HAVE changed things.

It always had before.

Not that Ginna had a lot of experience in that area. After her divorce, she hadn't been all that eager to enter the dating arena. Especially after listening to tales of woe from co-workers and clients.

It was easier when the only males in her life were her relatives and her dog.

But now something new had been added. Or rather, someone.

Zach only had to look at her and she wanted him. She even started to think exactly where she'd want him.

The shower had possibilities. The balcony if there wasn't the chance they'd be seen. She wasn't into public sex.

She hated each sunset because it meant one more day gone. It was getting close to the day when they'd be returning home.

She didn't want real life to intrude on what they shared.

Ginna didn't want to think it could happen. After all, they hadn't hopped into bed that first night, had they? Not even the first week. Instead, their kisses intensified until they almost burst into flames.

When she thought about it, she was amazed they'd held out as long as they had.

Each time they made love seemed even more magical than the previous time. Except each of those times reminded her of what she would never have. When he pulled out protection she wanted to tell him it wasn't necessary. He needn't fear she would become pregnant. She only wished it was an option for her. A choice she could make.

Instead of a choice made for her.

Even with their intense fascination with one another, they still found time to sightsee. The only difference was they no longer slept alone. When they did take time to sleep.

But one thought kept haunting her.

That day of reckoning was quickly approaching. She couldn't stop wondering if after returning to their everyday lives they'd discover other things that were more important than what they'd had here.

She told herself that didn't mean it would happen.

But what if it did?

ZACH SENSED that something was bothering Ginna. He just wasn't sure what it was.

He had an idea that part of it had to do with the fact that their vacations were just about over.

Was he in love with her?

What a question to ask himself!

How would she feel knowing he had kids? She'd said she wasn't planning on having any of her own. She was leaving that up to her siblings. But just because she wasn't planning on having children didn't mean she didn't like them. She'd said she did, after all.

By rights, he shouldn't want anything to do with a woman who wouldn't accept the twins.

He'd been with her when they wandered through shops and she picked up souvenirs for her nieces and nephew. When he picked up items for the twins, he let her assume they were for his nephew and a close friend's children. Damn, it left him feeling guilty.

To spend so much time choosing just the right items, you had to love children no matter what you said to the contrary.

She'd love the twins and he had a hunch they'd love her back.

Just as soon as he figured out how he was going to tell her about them.

Not exactly something you'd unexpectedly drop on a person.

But not now. Not when Ginna was lying so pliantly in his arms.

"Hey, you're thinking too hard." The object of his thoughts tapped him on the chest.

Right where his heart was.

They were sharing a lounger on his balcony. Ginna, wearing the shirt he'd earlier discarded and him feeling safe enough in his boxer shorts.

Damn, she made him laugh.

"We should be sleeping," he murmured, pressing a kiss to her temple.

"If we sleep, we miss all this." Ginna waved an arm to encompass the ocean beyond, the sound of waves breaking on the sand below a medley to their sated senses. "I want it to last forever." She burrowed against his chest. "Let's run off, find ourselves a deserted island and build a hut. We could run around naked all day," she threw in as further temptation.

He tightened his arms around her until she squealed.

"The naked part sounds good to me," he agreed. "At least, you getting naked sounds good. Admit it, you just don't want to get back on a plane."

"There is that." She twisted around to reach the wineglass they'd brought out with them. She gave him a sip, then took one herself.

"I called the airline. We'll be seated together," he said, using this as an inducement to get her on the plane the next day.

She snuggled further under his chin. "You are so good to me," she murmured. "One of those airplane-disaster movies was on TV earlier tonight. How do we know it wasn't an omen? We could steal a couple of sailboards and find that deserted island."

"That's why we didn't watch TV tonight." Zach grinned as he remembered just how he coaxed her away from the television. Not that she needed much coaxing once he started nibbling on her ear. He'd learned she was as sensitive there as she was in that hollow behind her left knee.

"Mmm." Obviously she remembered, too. "By staying up, morning will never come and we won't return to our respective lives and forget all about each other."

He didn't like the sound of that one bit. "I hate to tell you this, Ginna, but I'm not the love-'em-and-leave-'em type."

She ignored him. "I'd understand if it happened. After all, you'll be back to your magazine column and I'll be back doing hair." She didn't mention that they lived only two cities apart in Southern California, which was considered almost the same as living next door to each other.

"I have to say the more you put it that way—" Zach suddenly yelped. "Hey! That hurt!" He rubbed his chest where she'd pulled a hair.

"Don't be so agreeable when you should be arguing with me," she told him. "Or I'll really make you suffer."

"Sadistic woman," he said without heat. He suddenly froze. "Ginna, what are you doing?"

She reached up and kissed his chin. ''Oh, my darling, if you don't know, I must not be doing it right.''

''Oh, I think you're doing it right,'' he groaned as he thought his head was going to spin into outer space, ''but I guess a refresher course wouldn't hurt.''

Chapter Six

"Where're the pictures? Do not tell us you went all the way out there and didn't take any pictures!"

"Did you meet anyone?"

"Do you realize how many harmful UV rays you endured to get that tan? And I hate you for tanning so beautifully!"

"Let's get back to, Did Ginna meet anyone?"

"I've only been back for three days! I haven't picked up the pictures yet. I met a teenager named Tad. I used plenty of sunscreen when I was outside." Ginna dutifully replied to every question as she studied her appointment book.

"She met someone and not just someone named Tad. And I'm sorry, Ginna, but a guy named Tad sounds as if he's six years old," Nora announced. "And she's not sharing!"

Ginna turned around to face the staff of Steppin' Out.

"No, it's more than that," Cheryl announced. "Oh, my God, Ginna had sex! Really great sex. Mind-blowing sex. The kind of sex that makes a woman cry."

"What is with you women? Are you the sex police or something?" Ginna felt the damning heat rise in her neck.

"You did have sex!" Phoebe shrieked, pointing to her face. "What was he like? Does he live anywhere near here? Are you going to see him again, or was it one of those vacation flings you said you'd have?"

"Tell me it was the kind of hot raw sweaty sex we claim we wouldn't have. Of course, if the right man came along, we'd go for it," Nora said thoughtfully as if she was reliving a memory of her own.

"I don't know if I'll see him again." Ginna thought of Zach's phone number burning a hole in her bag.

"Just tell me you had incredible sex," Phoebe begged.

"Don't you have a facial to give?" she asked desperately as she looked toward the front door. She breathed a sigh of relief when she spied a familiar figure walk into the salon. "Sorry, ladies," she lied without a qualm, "my first appointment is here."

They drifted away to their own stations, but she knew her reprieve was a short one.

She wasn't ready to share Zach yet. She still missed him too much. Each night she went home and hoped to find a message from him on her answering machine. So far, the only messages were from friends and family. For now, she would settle for her memories.

"WE MISSED YOU, Daddy." Emma wrapped her arms around Zach's neck. Her lips smacked him on the cheek.

"I missed you, too, Peanut," he said, using his pet name for her. She smelled of milk and peanut butter from her morning toast.

"You should have taken Snooky with you," she told him, referring to the much beloved and battered bunny rabbit she slept with. "That way you wouldn't wake up in the middle of the night and be scared. You could hug Snooky and you'd feel better.''

Zach thought of what he had hugged in the middle of the night. He'd felt good then. Better than good.

''That's a nice thought, sweetie, but I think Snooky was happier staying here with you.'' He patted her on the bottom. ''Do you have everything for your day at preschool? Did you brush your teeth?''

''Uh-huh.'' Her head bobbed. ''Trey called Nick a bad name when we stayed at Aunt Lucie's,'' she confided.

Zach thought of a few names he could call his nephew, too, but he wasn't about to repeat them in front of his daughter. Nothing obscene. Miniature con artist was probably one of the worst.

''What did your Aunt Lucie say?'' he asked.

''She laughed and said Nick's been called worse, but she made Trey sit in Time-Out.''

''Good.'' He'd have to ask his sister what Trey said. Must have been a doozy if Lucie laughed. She was well-known for her insane sense of humor.

Zach always felt it was Lucie's sense of humor that kept her going.

He smiled at some of the memories of single men chasing after Lucie in the past few years. Sadly, most of them had run the other way when Nick revealed his Machiavellian side.

Zach would like to see his sister happy with a man. She deserved it after the bastard she'd married took off before Nick was born.

Both of them lost spouses before their children could have known their respective parents, but Zach knew Lucie got the raw end of the deal. He'd always regretted that Tony Donner hadn't been run over by a large truck.

Which was another reason why brother and sister remained so close over the years. He'd comforted Lucie when Tony left her high and dry. She'd been there to help him with the twins after they were born. He couldn't have asked for a better sister.

"Do we have to go to preschool today?" she asked, hugging him even tighter.

"It's Monday, so yes, you do." *He had to get to work on his column. Time to earn his living again.*

Emma's lower lip stuck out. "My tummy hurts," she whined.

"But Miss Mary reads *Mrs. Piggle Wiggle* on Mondays," he reminded her. "And you love *Mrs. Piggle Wiggle.*"

Emma laid her head against his shoulder. "Can I stay home?"

"You'll be fine once you get to school." He knew she was making the excuse because he'd been gone. Once they were at school, she'd forget all about her sore tummy.

"Daddy."

He turned to his son who stood in the hallway. Trey's mournful expression, green-tinged skin and the pungent mess on his clothing told the story.

"I throwed up." Trey's eyes were glassy with tears.

In keeping with the story that twins have to do everything together, Emma cried out once, then threw up all over Zach's shirtfront.

He was back in real life with a vengeance.

By that afternoon, Zach felt as if he'd been run over by a steamroller.

The twins' upset stomachs intensified. Luckily he was able to get them to their pediatrician that afternoon.

"Congratulations, Zach, they have the chicken pox,"

Dr. Gail Walker announced after examining each miserable child. "Put them in a warm bath when you get home and the spots will finish popping out."

Zach, who was seated next to the examination table, slumped.

"Both of them?" Now he felt like whining.

Real life, Zach.

"In a way, it's better both of them have it at the same time," she explained. "Do you really want to go through it one at a time when you can get it over with at once?"

He groaned.

"Dr. Gail," Trey moaned, clutching his stomach.

Gail was fast with a pan. Afterward she soothed him with a few words and gave him a hug.

"Don't let them scratch," she instructed. "Calamine lotion is still the best thing to use on the scabs, and you just have to let the disease run its course."

"Isn't there a shot you can give them?" Zach asked hopefully.

He hated himself when he saw the pity on her face.

"I realize two at once isn't going to be easy for you," she said. "Can Lucie help you out? Nick's already had the chicken pox, so there wouldn't be any problems there."

He shook his head. "No, I've got to be the adult here. Besides, she has enough going on in her life. I had the chicken pox and I was outside playing with the neighbor kids. Actually," he said thoughtfully, "the other mothers wanted me to infect their kids, so they could get it out of the way."

"That's how it's done," she said matter-of-factly. "If their temp goes up, or if anything out of the ordinary happens, give me a call. Otherwise, keep them comfortable, give them plenty of fluids and no scratching." She scribbled across a prescription pad. "If their nausea doesn't go away by tomorrow, try this." She handed the scrip to him.

"Isn't there something you can give *me?*" Zach asked as he picked Emma up in his arms while Trey hung on to his pants leg. "I love them. I really do. I guess I didn't think it would happen times two."

Gail laughed. "I hate to tell you this, Zach, but you aren't the first single parent to go through this and you won't be the last."

"Daddy, I wanna go to bed," Emma whined in his ear.

"Okay, Peanut, we're going home and then it's to bed with both of you."

Just as the doctor predicted, by nighttime, courtesy of a warm bath, the twins were covered with pink and red spots. And they were both thoroughly miserable.

They didn't want to sleep in their own room. They wanted to be with him. Their ears hurt. They seemed to throw up every hour on the hour, and Trey ran a low fever around midnight.

Zach shared his bed with an overly warm small body on either side of him. He thought of another warm body he'd rather have in his bed. Instead of indulging himself in some nice X-rated fantasies, he cuddled two fractious children, read to them, brought them drinks of water and forgot all about getting any sleep.

For two children who'd slept the night through as babies, never got colic or anything else babies got, they were now making up for it big time, demanding their share of attention.

Zach had no time to shave, managed to shower in two minutes, poached eggs to put on toast and read stories until he was hoarse. Sleep was something he indulged in when the twins allowed it.

When one was asleep, the other was awake and whined for Daddy to make things better. He slid his socks on their hands so they couldn't scratch their scabs. He joked that they could play connect the dots, but they didn't find it funny.

He mentally wrote his column on how Dad survived twins having the chicken pox at the same time.

Real life, Zach.

ONE STEP IN FRONT of the other. Keep your breathing even.

Don't think about him.

"Damn!"

Casper barked and looked up at Ginna as if scolding her.

"Don't look at me that way. You've heard worse," she said grimly, and quickened her pace.

The white German shepherd easily kept up with her. There was nothing he liked better in the mornings than to take one of the jogging paths in the nearby park. He wasn't sure why his mistress was taking longer runs in the morning, but he wasn't complaining.

"Men are scum, Casp," Ginna told him. "I should have known better than to believe his speech about how he doesn't love them and leave them. You, I can trust. You won't abandon me even if you meet a perky little poodle." The dog's eyes were pleading when they looked up at her. "Say all you want. That surgery was in your best interests. That way we don't have to worry about paternity suits."

By the time they returned to the house, Ginna was dripping with sweat and Casper was panting. The dog immediately headed for his water bowl while she dropped onto a kitchen chair.

Since this was her late day, she didn't have to worry about the time. She could sit in the chair and feel sorry for herself all morning if she wanted to.

But if she was truly honest with herself, that wasn't what she wanted.

She wanted to pick up the phone and call Zach. No, she wanted Zach to pick up the damn phone and call her!

Ginna was a woman of the new millennium, but there were things she still liked to think men should do.

He'd probably forgotten her the minute they parted at the airport. He'd told her he'd call her, and so far, there hadn't even been a Dear Jane phone call.

Zach had obviously returned to his old life, and she was nothing more than a vacation memory that would fade with time.

Denny had left her because she couldn't give him a child. Zach left her because… She had no idea why he left her. That hurt even more than Denny's betrayal, because she hadn't been told what her defect was where Zach was concerned.

On second thought, she wanted him to suffer. A lot. Viciously.

She wasn't sure how, but given time, she knew she could come up with something good.

As if sensing his mistress's sorrow, Casper got up and walked over to her, laying his head in her lap. He whined to catch her attention. She looked down and smiled. She put her hands on either side of his face and leaned down, rubbing her cheek against his soft fur.

"At least you don't snore," she murmured.

If she wasn't allowed to sit here and feel sorry for

herself, she'd do the next-best thing. She knew the ingredients were on hand, and there was nothing better than just-out-of-the-oven chocolate-chip oatmeal cookies.

"They're healthy," she reminded her co-workers as she set the platter on a table in the back of the salon a few hours later. "Oatmeal lowers cholesterol."

"It's the chocolate chips that make them good." Nora swiped a cookie on her way out of the room. She stopped and looked at Ginna. "Are you okay?"

"Three-mile run with Casper," she said brightly.

"It's just that you've been back for more than two weeks and, well…" She paused, unsure whether or not to forge ahead. "Well…" She stopped again.

"I had my vacation fling," Ginna told her. "I said I was going out there to have fun and I did."

Nora looked unconvinced by her words, but knowing she wouldn't hear anything more, she left.

Ginna checked her appointment book and frowned.

"Darcy, why did you book an appointment at this time?" she asked the receptionist. "That's later than I normally work tonight."

"He said he really needed a haircut and you had been recommended," she explained.

Ginna looked at the name penciled in. *Zachary.*

It didn't mean he was *her* Zachary. It was probably someone's last name.

"Did he say who recommended me?"

"No."

"Okay," she said finally. "But please, next time, call me first." She returned to her station. She picked up a few pins and with a well-practiced twist, pinned her hair on top of her head. "Nora?" The hairdresser next to her looked over. "Would you have time this afternoon to do something with my hair?"

"Sure, about three."

Ginna checked her book. "Sounds good to me."

It was time for a change.

IT WAS THE FIRST DAY Zach had been out of the house for almost two weeks.

The twins were back in preschool, Mrs. Clover, his cleaning woman, had come in for the first time in four-teen days, lamented over the state of the house and set to work. He'd shut himself up in his office to work. But instead of working on his column, he sat there day-dreaming about Ginna.

He thought about just calling her. And say what? That he hadn't been able to call her earlier because he'd been nursing two children through the chicken pox?

He decided to take the coward's way out. He called the salon and managed to charm a haircut appointment out of the receptionist, even though she told him Ginna normally didn't take appointments that late.

He spent a long time in the shower, gloried in the clean clothes Mrs. Clover had hung in his closet and waited until it was time to head for the Steppin' Out Salon.

Considering he normally had his hair cut at Rupert's Barbershop, the salon was a new experience for him. At least he wasn't the only male client in there, he noticed with relief upon his arrival.

He studied the interior after he'd given his name to the receptionist and was told to be seated. Ginna would be with him in a few moments. Black-and-white-tile floor, music that inspired dancing and an energy in the air that was infectious.

He saw Ginna before she saw him.

What the hell did she do to her hair?

She was dressed in a white lacy sleeveless top and a short black skirt that displayed those legs he fondly remembered wrapped around him. Sheer black hose and high heels. Damn, she was wearing those high heels that made her legs go on forever.

But what he really noticed was the lack of shoulder-length curls he'd played with many a time when they'd been together.

Inches had been cut off and the curls were replaced with a smooth curve that swung against her cheek. One side was clipped back behind her ear.

He knew to the second when she saw him. She stopped short and just looked at him. For a moment he was positive those beautiful blue eyes were going to turn him into an icicle.

"Mr. Zachary?" she drawled with a faint hint of sarcasm.

"I was afraid if you knew it was me, you'd refuse the appointment," he said candidly.

"You're probably right," she said just as candidly. "Come on back." She sat him in a chair and wrapped a cloth around his neck. "Just a haircut?" Her fingers combed through his hair, but he felt it was more clinical than the other times she'd done it.

"Something else you'd suggest?"

"It's pretty dry. A good conditioning treatment wouldn't hurt," she said crisply, sounding as if she was talking to a perfect stranger. "I'll take you back for a shampoo, then we'll go from there. Kim," she called out, "would you shampoo Mr. Stone please, then put on a conditioning pack?"

The shampoo girl nodded and directed Zach to follow her.

Ginna decided if she could get through this next hour, she could get through anything.

Why was he here?

She looked down at her hands. They were shaking.

She could do this. She could treat him as if he was nothing more than a casual acquaintance. So what if he'd seen her naked and she'd seen him naked. *Oh, my God!* The man made her feel as if the Fourth of July had gone off inside her body, and she was determined to stand here and cut his hair as if nothing had happened?

She jumped when a hand landed on her shoulder.

"If I could go on vacation and meet someone like him, I'd be gone tomorrow," Nora murmured.

"I don't know what you mean," Ginna lied.

"Honey, you looked at that man as if he was one of those éclairs you're so crazy about," she told her. "And the way he looked at you?" She fanned her face. "We're talking hot stuff here. I'm amazed the two of you didn't go up in flames when you looked at each other. I am so jealous."

"Oh, sure, and that's why he hasn't called once," she said between clenched teeth.

Nora nodded knowingly. "I had a feeling that was him. I'd say if he hasn't called you, it's for a good reason. Give him a chance before you stab him with those scissors, okay?"

"I'll think about it," Ginna said grimly. She felt more composed when Kim returned Zach to her.

"Ginna—" he began.

"I'd say you need more than a trim," she said brightly, combing this way and that to see how his hair lay.

He tried a bit more forcefully. "Gin—"

"Some serious shaping needed here."

He captured her wrist. "There was a medical emergency in my family," he said rapidly. "I wanted to call you. God, I wanted you so badly." His voice broke.

She paused long enough to get a good look at him. A nick on his chin where he must have cut himself shaving. Bloodshot eyes. Sleep hadn't been one of his activities lately. He looked exhausted. Before thinking, she blurted out her thoughts.

"You look terrible."

He smiled wanly. "Thanks. Now I know my mirror wasn't lying." His fingers caressed her wrist. "I missed you."

"No, you didn't."

"The hell I didn't. I missed you wrapping yourself around me at night," he kept on relentlessly. "I missed your shower fogging up the mirror while I tried to shave. I missed your cute little hip wiggles when you put on your makeup. I missed *you*."

"You were supposed to forget about me," she whispered. "Go on with your life."

"The hell I was," he said furiously, but keeping his voice low. "Tell me you didn't think about me."

"I didn't think about you."

His eyes gleamed. "Liar."

"Zach, I'm holding a sharp pair of scissors here," she said in a low and extremely seductive voice. "Not exactly a good time to call me a liar."

He released her wrist. "Okay, but if you cut my ear off, you're not getting a tip."

Ginna combed her fingers through his wet hair, watching the strands curl around her fingertips. It wasn't easy for her to think as a hairdresser when the last time she'd combed her fingers through his hair, they were both naked. Her motions slowed. She lifted her eyes, glanced at him in the mirror. His gaze was intent on her face.

"The conditioner helped," she said, forcing herself back to her professional persona. "You should think about using one on a regular basis. You've got dry ends, but those will be trimmed today."

"I noticed my hair had gotten lighter in the past month or so."

"You were in a lot of sun, so it's natural there'd be a bleaching effect," she explained. "Didn't Rupert ever tell you about sun damage?"

"You remembered his name," he murmured.

She ignored his comment. Instead, she combed strands, held them up and began cutting.

Zach, realizing that now might not a good time to say anything provocative, remained quiet and didn't move a muscle.

"I haven't stabbed a client in months. You can relax," she murmured.

"I wanted to call you every night," he said, deciding to take the plunge.

His reply was the quiet snip of scissors.

"I missed having you in bed with me."

"My dog takes up the other half of the bed very nicely. Get a puppy."

"I'd rather have you."

"That was then. This is now. Real life, Zach," she mocked him.

He winced at her choice of words, ones that had been haunting him for the past couple of weeks.

He remained silent during the rest of his haircut.

When she'd finished, Ginna picked up a hairdryer and switched it on. In no time, his hair was dry and styled.

Zach studied his reflection. The style wasn't much different from the way he normally wore his hair, but he could see subtle differences.

"How come it looks the same but doesn't?" he asked.

"The difference comes from the cut," she replied as she set down the dryer.

Zach pulled out his wallet.

She shook her head. "If I'd had my scissors with me in Hawaii, I would have done it then."

"This is also how you make your living." He pulled bills out.

"Zach, no," she said firmly.

"Then let me take you to dinner."

Out of the corner of his eye he could see in the mirror the hairdresser next to them. She'd obviously been eavesdropping on their conversation. Her head was bobbing up and down and her mouth was shaping the words *do it!*

He decided to press the issue when he noticed Ginna's hesitation.

"Please."

Ginna closed her eyes. "Give me some time to clean up."

Zach knew when to back off. He nodded and headed back to the reception area.

"He is adorable!" Nora whispered the minute Zach was out of earshot. "If you don't want him, can I have a try?"

Ginna glared at her friend. "No!"

Nora grinned. "I rest my case. You're not as mad at him as he thinks you are."

"No," she reluctantly admitted. "But that doesn't mean he has to know that right away, does it?"

Nora chuckled. "Someday you and I are going out to

lunch and you are going to tell me just what went on out there.''

Ginna's good humor surfaced. ''Sorry, sweetie, you'll just have to use your imagination.'' She glanced in the mirror and applied fresh lipstick.

''Don't be sorry. I have a very good imagination.''

Chapter Seven

Zach asked Ginna for restaurant recommendations in the area. She suggested a place that was within walking distance of the salon.

As they moved down the sidewalk, she noticed he kept glancing at her.

"What?" she asked, still not ready to forgive him for not calling her. She, above all, understood family obligations. But a tiny selfish part of her wanted him to have taken even two minutes to call her and explain the situation.

"You cut your hair."

Ginna shrugged. "It was time for a change." It wasn't as easy as she'd thought to put on an uninterested front.

Zach was a welcome sight even if she could see the signs of weariness in his manner. He had the appearance of a man who hadn't had a good night's sleep in some time.

Two weeks, perhaps?

She quickly looked away.

"You're not going to make it easy for me, are you," he said, holding the restaurant door open for her.

"I've been busy catching up," she said, preferring not to answer him. "I'm sure you've been busy, too."

"Oh, yeah," he murmured, before moving forward to request a table for two. "Had a couple surprises I hadn't counted on."

They were seated immediately. They declined a before-dinner drink and were left with their menus.

"Everything here is good," she told him as she opened her menu.

"Red meat sounds good to me."

Ginna frowned at him. "Try fish, instead. I'll have the grilled chicken breast, rice pilaf and iced tea," she told the waitress as she handed her the menu.

"Sirloin, medium rare, baked potato," Zach said with a warm smile. "And coffee."

The moment they were left alone, he turned back to Ginna.

"As you said, it's back to real life," he said. "Did your dog miss you?"

"When I first picked Casper up at my parents, I wasn't too sure," she said, relieved Zach was keeping their conversation impersonal. "I have an idea they spoiled him rotten. Too many treats, sleeping on the couch. Probably even let him eat dinner at the table. My mother claims his manners are better than my dad's. I think she was exaggerating a little, but then, with my dad, you never can be too sure." She looked up and smiled at the waitress as she placed the glass of iced tea in front of her. "I let him know his vacation was over. Back to morning runs. Treats at specified times only and his food dish remains on the kitchen floor."

"Boy, you're a tough dog mom."

"I have to be." She sipped her drink. "If I wasn't, he'd walk all over me."

Zach grinned. "So instead, he runs with you?"

"I like to run in the mornings. About two years ago,

there were some assaults on women joggers on the paths I took. For a while, I drove out to my parents' house, started running on the back trails there and took their dog with me. When she had puppies, I took one look at Casper and it was love at first sight,'' she said. ''When he was old enough and big enough, I returned to my old running trail.''

''Did they ever catch the guy?'' he asked.

''More like he did it to himself.'' She chuckled. ''He made the mistake of trying to drag a female marine off into the brush. She beat the crap out of him. He was begging for the cops to arrest him. By then, more women were running with dogs or in groups. There hasn't been an assault there since.''

''Never mess with a woman who has survival skills.'' Zach picked up his coffee cup. ''You know, after those two weeks, coming back home was a major culture shock. Rush hour. Car alarms going off at odd hours. Everyone in a hurry to get somewhere.''

Ginna nodded. ''I know. The first morning I was home I realized I had no coffee in the house. Not a good thing at all where I'm concerned. And it wasn't as if I could call down and order from room service. I had to get dressed, or at least look dressed, so I could run out for coffee. In the end, I went over to one of my brothers' houses and bummed coffee off them.''

''I miss the sound of the ocean.''

''The band in the lounge.''

''Finding sand in my clothes.''

''Not having to wear shoes.''

Zach held up his finger to emphasize he had the ultimate complaint. ''Telemarketers.''

''At dinnertime!'' She laughed.

''Anytime.''

Just like that, they were once again in sync. The two weeks apart dissolved as if they'd never happened.

After dinner, they shared cheesecake and coffee and kept on talking.

Zach was surprised when he realized just how late it was. He hadn't planned on staying out this late. Good thing Lucie was keeping the twins for the night.

"I can't believe the hour," Ginna exclaimed, glancing at her watch. "Casper has a doggie door, but he doesn't like to use it unless it's absolutely necessary. He got stuck in it once. Not to mention he'll be looking for his dinner."

Zach asked the waitress for the bill and quickly settled it.

"Where do you park?" he asked.

"All of us have parking behind the spa," she explained. "It's well lit, so we've never worried going out there at night."

"I'll still walk you back there."

"What about you?"

"I'm out in front."

Ginna headed for a gleaming black 1966 Mustang. She clicked a remote and heard the chirp of her car alarm.

Zach couldn't stop staring at the car. "I think I'm in love."

"You men," she said, opening the driver's door and tossing her bag onto the passenger seat. "If you like this, you would have loved my brother Brian's Corvette convertible. He sold it when he became a new daddy. Mark and Jeff cried when they found out he'd done that. I told you my dad restored classic automobiles. This was one of his babies."

"Knowing about it and seeing the results are two different things." He ran his hand lovingly along the fender.

He stopped when he was next to her. He started to dip his head, then stopped just before his mouth brushed hers.

"I think I should tell you I won't be as easy this time around."

Ginna laughed out loud. "As if you were before."

Her laughter was cut off by his mouth covering hers. Her arms lifted, circling his neck as she angled her body against his.

Their tongues tangled as their bodies reacquainted themselves.

"Ever make love in the back seat of a Mustang?" Zach asked her.

"Ever have your back broken?" she replied.

"Because of the question or because of the seat?" He nibbled his way along her jawline.

"You figure it out for yourself." She pushed up the hem of his forest-green polo shirt. She purred with delight at the feel of his warm skin.

"How about the hood?" He bumped his hip against hers.

Sanity reared its ugly head as Ginna pulled back. "I have a hungry dog to feed." Her breath came in short gasps. "Besides, I want to stay mad at you for a while longer."

Zach pulled her back in his arms and kissed her until they were both clutching at each other. When he stepped back, he kept hold of her arms.

"Still mad at me?"

"Yes." She didn't sound one-quarter as convincing as she had before.

He started toward her again. She thrust out her hands in a stop action.

"Okay, you made your point." She practically pressed herself against her car. "I have to go now."

"I want to see you again," Zach told her.

"I work the next two evenings," she replied.

He looked thoughtful as if he was mentally reviewing his calendar. "How about brunch on Sunday?"

She smiled. "I'd like that."

"I'll pick you up at ten."

She nodded. She ducked into her car, rummaged through her bag and pulled out a business card and pen. She wrote her home address on the back and handed it to him.

Zach took advantage of the moment to steal another kiss, which would have led to more if they hadn't heard voices in the distance.

"Go," she ordered, pushing him off.

"Hey." He stopped her before she closed the car door completely. She looked at him. He gestured to his head. "You give great hair."

Ginna rolled her eyes, closed the door and drove off.

Zach whistled under his breath as he walked around to the front of the building.

As long as the twins remained healthy, he'd be just fine.

"EVERYONE'S COMING OVER Sunday for a barbecue," Cathy Walker told her daughter as she pulled a muffin pan out of the oven. "You can make it, can't you?"

"Actually, no, I can't. I have plans." Ginna should have known stopping by her parents' house wasn't a good idea. But she knew Thursday was her mother's day to bake, and her caramel pecan rolls were better than anything sold in a bakery. By the time she arrived, two pans of rolls were cooling on the counter, along with freshly baked loaves of coconut bread and orange bread.

The Walker household was always filled with hungry men due to Lou Walker's garage being on the property. He refused to retire and continued bringing classic cars back to life. Friends and clients alike were known to stop off at the kitchen to beg for a muffin or a cinnamon roll and a cup of coffee. Lou complained no one came to see him—they came to eat his wife's cooking.

Ginna sat at the breakfast bar with her hands cradling a large mug detailed with bright lettering stating Mechanics Know Their Parts. She nibbled on a still-warm caramel pecan roll.

Cathy poured coffee into a mug and sat on the stool next to her daughter. "Anyone we know?"

"No," Ginna said promptly.

"Do we get to meet him?" her mom probed.

"Only if he passes the background investigation to make sure he doesn't have a criminal record," Ginna said flippantly.

Cathy waved her hand airily. "One little mistake."

"Little mistake? Mom, the guy was wanted for fraud in three states." She reminded her mother of the man Cathy deemed perfect for her oldest daughter. "Not to mention, he always made the worst jokes." Ginna wrinkled her nose in memory.

"Blame your father. Steve was here to buy that Nash your father was selling. He knew cars. Your dad was in love on your behalf."

"He fell out of love fast when he found out the check Steve gave him was no good." Ginna licked her fingers. She looked around. "Didn't you make any cookies this morning?"

"Not today." Cathy studied her daughter. "You're more cheerful than you were after you got back from your trip. Oh, you were happy enough when you got back, but after that first week…" Her voice fell off. She leaned forward and peered into her daughter's face. "Either you met someone new or you saw the man you met in Hawaii."

"What are you? The head of one of those psychic networks?" Ginna reared back. "Why don't you do this with Nikki?"

"She's dating a very nice medical student. He's going to specialize in cardiology, so for now, she's off the hook." Cathy didn't take her eyes off her daughter. "Which is it?"

"Zach." Ginna supplied the one word she hoped would call her mother off. The moment she said the name, she realized her mistake.

Cathy's face lit up. "That's who you met in Hawaii. That settles it, then—you need to bring him on Sunday."

"No way," Ginna said. "He's not ready to meet the piranhas I call Dad and brothers. Not to mention Mother," she muttered, reaching for another roll.

Cathy smoothly slid the pan out of Ginna's reach.

"It's too soon," Ginna argued, her hand still outstretched. "In Hawaii, it was like something out of a movie. Two people meet on a plane, find they have a lot in common, end up at the same hotel, and something develops. But now they're back home. Their jobs take precedence, as does real life. What they saw in each other out there might not be the same here."

"He already doesn't sound at all like Denny," Cathy said. "Thank God."

"No one's like Denny," Ginna said with heartfelt sincerity.

Cathy reached across and covered Ginna's hand with her own. "He was wrong, dear. None of it was your fault."

Ginna blinked rapidly to hold back the tears that threatened to fall. Just the memory was enough to bring back a remembrance of times better left forgotten.

"That's not what the doctors said." She looked away.

"That I can't believe," Cathy protested.

"Then you tell me how Denny's wife has one child by him and another on the way when I couldn't get pregnant no matter what?" Ginna demanded. "We had the tests done, Mom. And as Denny said, it was me. Not him."

Her mother's comment on Denny's opinion was less than favorable.

"Mom!" Ginna was alternately shocked and amused at her mother's language.

Cathy brought the pan back within reaching distance.

"All right, but you'll have to bring Zach out here sooner or later."

Ginna knew it, but she still wanted to keep Zach to herself for a while longer.

"AREN'T YOU COMING with us?" Emma asked her father as she watched him knot his tie. She was bouncing up and down in the middle of his bed, her arms waving with her movements.

"That is not a trampoline," he said firmly. "And no, sweetie, your aunt Lucie and Nick are taking you and Trey out for lunch, then you're going to see that Disney movie you wanted to see. You're going to have lots of fun."

Emma dropped onto the bed. Her legs stuck straight

out as she fiddled with the laces on her Winnie the Pooh tennis shoes.

"We have fun with you, too," she said, resting soulful eyes on her father in a look guaranteed to inspire guilt.

Used to his daughter's machinations, Zach felt no guilt. Not when Lucie, the moment he asked if she wouldn't mind watching the kids today, had volunteered to take them to lunch and a movie the twins had wanted to see since before they'd gotten sick.

"We don't want you to be by yourself, Daddy," Emma went on.

"I won't be, Peanut. I'm seeing a friend today."

"Your girlfriend?"

He figured he could blame Lucie for that question. "Just a friend."

"If you had a girlfriend, we could all go to the zoo and to the park," Emma went on. "And she could take me to the store and find me clothes for kindergarten." She warmed to her favorite subject. For her, entering kindergarten was the same as entering a top university was for an eighteen-year-old.

Trey wasn't as excited about the prospect. He had a crush on his preschool teacher and wanted to stay where he was.

"I don't do so bad finding you clothes," Zach pointed out. "And you were the one who told me your aunt Lucie found that pink dress for you."

"But she's my aunt!" she said as if that made all the difference in the world. "You know what we need, Daddy? We need a mommy."

His collar suddenly started suffocating him. "I think we do pretty good on our own." But that didn't stop him thinking about Ginna, who spoke so warmly about her own family. With his and Lucie's brother.

Emma scooted forward and slid off the end of the bed. "Well, Daddy—" she switched to a long-suffering voice he swore echoed her aunt Lucie's "—you better find me a mom in time for me to learn makeup and all the big-girl stuff."

Zach thought about what type of "big-girl stuff" was going to creep into his daughter's life over the next twenty years. He was finding it impossible to breathe. He loosened his collar.

He could see it now. His telling Ginna about the twins.

I have a daughter who's four going on thirty-five and a four-year-old son who's going on four and a half.

"Get your pack," he wheezed. "We're leaving for Aunt Lucie's."

He watched her saunter out of his bedroom. His little girl was growing up way too fast. He only hoped he'd survive her formative years.

GINNA BURST OUT laughing when she opened the door and found Zach standing there holding a white teddy bear, a tire gauge tied to its paws with red ribbon.

"Romantic enough?" Zach asked, handing her the bear.

"And practical at the same time," she said, taking the bear out of his hands. "Thank you."

"That's a top-of-the-line tire gauge," he said. "Only the best for you."

"I can see." She was visibly impressed. "Would you like to come in?"

The minute Zach crossed the threshold a white German shepherd moved in front of him. The dog's expression wasn't welcoming.

"This is Casper," Ginna said, keeping her hand resting on the dog's head. "Casper, say hello."

The dog lifted a paw, which Zach took cautiously.

Casper gave him his best "I'm watching you" expression as he dutifully backed up. To prove it, he didn't take his gaze off Zach.

"I don't think he likes me," Zach said, keeping a wary eye on the canine.

"Casper loves everyone," Ginna insisted, leaning down to hug the dog. "I'll just be a second." She disappeared toward the back of the house.

"So, you into football, Casper?" Zach asked.

The low rumble coming from his throat wasn't reassuring.

Ginna returned carrying a lilac-colored short-sleeved sweater that she pulled on over her lilac-print strapless dress.

"I'm sorry you had to wait," she apologized, bending down to slip on her shoes. "It's just been one of those mornings."

"No problem." *Not when he got to watch her put on another pair of sexy high heels.*

He'd never considered high-heeled shoes sexy until he saw them on Ginna.

Her loose curls were pulled back with lilac-colored pearlized clips. A light floral cologne drifted in his direction.

She picked up a small lilac leather bag and slung the narrow strap over her shoulder. She murmured something to the dog, who shot Zach a look filled with suspicion.

"What do you have planned, my handsome Mr. Stone?" she asked him, tucking her arm through his as he walked her to his shiny red Pathfinder.

"Not the beach," was all he told her as he helped her into the vehicle.

She reached out and straightened the collar of his dusty teal-colored polo shirt, which he'd tucked into khaki-colored pants.

He grinned at her. She wrinkled her nose.

"Can I help it if I can't keep my hands off you?" she quipped.

"Honey, that goes for both of us."

As he rounded the hood to the driver's side, he was grateful he had made the time to get the truck washed before picking Ginna up. He had also taken out the kids seats then ensured there were no toys hiding in the back or petrified French fries lurking under the seats.

"Pity, I haven't been to the beach in such a long time." She gazed at him under the cover of her lashes. "Now you have me curious."

"I think you'll like it, but I'll warn you now it's a bit of a drive."

She buckled her seat belt and turned partway so she could face him.

"Good, then you can tell me what you've been writing for your column," she said brightly. "Did you remember what I told you?"

"More than you'll ever know," he replied.

Under Ginna's coaxing, he talked about some of the subjects he'd touched on without mentioning the column he'd written about his experience with the twins and the chicken pox. He'd managed to work the conversation around to her.

"My parents are having a family barbecue today," she said.

"And you escaped?" he teased.

"I was very lucky," Ginna replied. "There's nothing like having screaming kids run rings around you to make your day totally insane."

"I thought it only got insane if they screamed in your ear," Zach said carefully.

"My brother and sister-in-law have twin girls. When they get going, we have stereo screaming." She chuckled. "Please, don't get me wrong. I love them dearly, but as I explain to Jeff and Abby, I am their aunt. I'm the one who feeds them sugar, gives them noisy toys and then sends them home to Mom and Dad."

Zach winced. "I thought that job belonged to the grandparents."

"Mine do their share. But they also have other ways to entertain the kids. The girls love to spend time with their grandpa when he shows them how to change an oil filter. After their grandma scrubs the grease off them, she lets them help her bake cookies."

"I see. Equal opportunity entertainment," Zach said with approval.

During the drive, he got her talking some more about her family. From everything she said, it was obvious she was very close to them.

Ginna exclaimed in delight as they drove through rows of grapevines and up a hill where a large sprawling old-fashioned house dominated the property.

"This is fantastic," she said as he helped her out.

"Wait," he told her as they climbed the steps to the front door, which was a design of grape clusters set in stained glass.

A silver-haired woman greeted them with a broad smile as Zach gave his name. She led them through several large rooms set up for dining. She didn't halt until they were standing outside on a shaded patio. A table was set up on the edge of the patio, which overlooked a valley of grapevines.

Ginna immediately walked to the edge to look out.

She spun on her heel to face Zach. The joy lighting her face told him everything he needed to know.

"How did you find out about this place?" she asked as he seated her at the table.

"A friend told me about it," he replied. "They only serve so many people on the weekend, and I lucked out getting the patio table." *Along with some major begging and the fact that the owner was a fan of his column.* "Our meal is at the mercy of the chef's whims."

Her expression was elated as she looked around. She smiled at the waiter who brought out mimosas for them. He left a basket filled with croissants and muffins with the explanation he would be bringing them some fresh fruit.

"And to think all I did was cut your hair." She smiled at him.

"All right, pat yourself on the back," he said with a mock long-suffering sigh. "I wash it, blow it dry and it falls into place."

"What can I say? When you go to an expert, you get professional hair." She gave a regal nod of the head. Her eyes lit up when a large bowl of fruit was placed between them. She chose a strawberry and leaned across the table to brush it across his lips. He obediently opened his mouth and bit down. She took the uneaten half and popped it into her mouth. When she offered him a piece of melon, his lips brushed her fingertips this time. She smiled and ate what he didn't. She followed it with a bit of buttered croissant.

"Excellent choice, Mr. Stone," she murmured, taking a bite of a muffin.

Ginna almost purred when plates of eggs Benedict were placed in front of them. She smiled her thanks at the waiter as he also placed another mimosa by her plate.

"Until I met you, I thought women only picked at their food," Zach said.

She shook her head. "And miss out on wonderful food like this? I don't think so." She slipped off her sweater, then smiled as the waiter gallantly draped it over the back of her chair.

Zach attempted to smile, but he had trouble holding it. He wasn't sure he wanted anyone else admiring Ginna's naked shoulders. A shaft of sunlight chased its way across the table to finally settle on her.

Dammit, it would be so easy to fall in love with this woman.

She seemed to know when to make conversation and when to be quiet. She was sincerely interested in other people. He thought of teasing her that she'd probably sit down and have a talk with the devil if she was given a chance.

"It's like another world out here," she commented, sipping her mimosa. "This house was probably built a good hundred years ago. The vineyards have probably been here even longer. I could stay here forever." She looked out, then laughed softly. "Look, Zach." She gestured.

His gaze followed her arm and saw what had caught her attention—a brilliantly colored hot-air balloon seemed to hover over the vineyard before air currents carried it away.

"I heard they usually go up at dawn. And I know how much you like to sleep late," he teased.

"I don't recall you exactly rolling out of bed too early," she retorted, stabbing another strawberry with her fork.

They took their time with their meal, all the while enjoying the view and each other. When finished, they strolled hand in hand along paths that afforded them views of the valley below.

At one point, Ginna turned to Zach and linked her arms around his neck. Her face glowed with happiness and too many mimosas.

"Thank you," she whispered, reaching up to kiss him lightly on the mouth. "You have given me one of the most beautiful days in my life." She kissed him again, but this time he held her against him.

Yep, he was definitely falling in love with this woman.

Chapter Eight

"It all went by too fast," Ginna said with a sigh as Zach drove down the road, leaving the vineyard behind. She fingered the heavy green bottle that had been presented to them when they left. "Wasn't that nice of the restaurant's owner to give us a bottle of champagne?" Ginna asked, snuggling down in the leather seat. "He said he likes your column. I'm sorry, I still haven't read it. I guess I'll have to start reading it." She hummed under her breath.

"It all has to do with guy stuff," Zach warned her. "Not exactly interesting reading for women."

"That's all right. I really should read it. That way, I can make sure you took my advice on what's romantic and what's not. It's just too bad it's in a magazine geared for men." She continued humming softly along with the radio.

"I guess it does sound odd. Writing a column for men that's featured in a men's magazine," he said, tongue in cheek.

"There are women interested in reading what men have to say about us," she informed him. "You can't tell me that you men aren't interested in reading what we women have to say about your sex."

"Sex in general, or the male sex in particular?"

Ginna shot him a "Behave" look. "Don't think you can easily confuse me. I only have a mild buzz. The orange juice helped keep the champagne at bay. Vitamin C and all that." She waved her hands for emphasis. "I know you talked some about your column when we were in Hawaii, but I feel as though there's more to it."

"There is." Since the day had started to cool off, Zach turned on the heater, adjusting the vents to blow gently on Ginna.

She leaned forward. "I knew it! Now you have to tell all."

She noticed a peculiar expression cross his face. If she'd had her wits about her, she would have tried to dig in deep with more probing questions.

"A publisher approached me about my column," Zach said finally.

"Publisher, as in book?" she asked.

He nodded. "They don't want me to just compile my past columns. They'd like me to expand on them. Maybe use one column subject for each chapter."

"On single men living in today's world," she clarified. "I guess it's only fair since there're so many books out there on single women living in today's world. But what makes yours unique? Isn't that what they look for? Something that's different from the others on the market?"

He thought for a moment. "Maybe I'll just let you read some of my columns. They'll tell you more than I could."

She sat back. "I look forward to it. Are you going to write a column about today?"

Zach shook his head. "No way. Some things aren't meant for public consumption. But I'm tempted to write about how to handle a lady's dog when said dog isn't too polite.''

"Casper didn't bite you, did he?'' She looked worried.

"No, thank God!"

"Casper takes the role of my protector very seriously,'' she explained. "I know it's probably been a while since you read *Peter Pan,* but Casper would have made a good Nana, the nursemaid.''

"Except Casper is an athletic German shepherd while Nana was a large and fluffy St. Bernard,'' he said.

She was impressed he was familiar with the popular children's story, then remembered he'd said he had a young nephew. She couldn't imagine any boy not wishing for a life where he didn't have to grow up.

Except Zach had grown up very nicely.

Instead of doing the obvious of taking her to a restaurant on the beach where he could play on her memories of Hawaii, he'd done the exact opposite. It must have taken him time to find something as original as the elegant restaurant set among the vineyards.

Dining on the sunlit patio had been private, their waiter only appearing when they needed him.

She was sated with good food and mimosas.

A day she would have recorded in a diary if she still kept one.

Instead, she'd tuck today in her memory banks and bring it out on days when she needed the memory.

Zach was so different than any other man she'd dated in the past. Most importantly, he would never lie to her.

"ARE YOU SAYING he brought you a teddy bear holding a tire gauge?'' Nora said as the two women stepped down into the bubbling mineral pool in the rear of the spa.

Since the salon and spa were closed on Mondays, the employees took advantage of the amenities and shared services on that day.

Today Ginna had come in to give Nora a weave and later relax with a massage from Phoebe.

They sat on the curved bench in a corner of the warm pool while Ginna told her friend about her brunch with Zach.

"He's too perfect," Nora declared. "There has to be something wrong. You said his clothes are clean and they actually match. His truck was freshly washed. No fast-food wrappers in sight. He took you to this incredible place for a brunch that sounds fantastic."

"Tasted even better," Ginna said, rolling a towel behind her head so she could rest it against the side of the rectangular pool. "The mimosas were—" she waved her hand languidly in the air as she searched for just the right word "—incredible. Everything else was beyond that."

"Well, what I saw was good," Nora said. "If I'd gone to Hawaii, I would have ended up with someone who looked like Kermit the frog."

"That last guy you dated sounded like Kermit," Ginna joked, then shrieked when Nora splashed water at her. "I'd be careful if I were you," she warned. "I'm not the one whose hair was just done."

Nora patted the tousled curls pinned to the top of her head.

"I'm just hoping my date tonight is a prince and not a frog," she said.

"Since I created a coiffure masterpiece, he better take

you someplace befitting your beautiful self," Ginna told her.

"I'll be sure to tell him you said that," Nora joked. "What about you, Gin? Do you think Zach's The One?"

Ginna shrugged. "I'm afraid to think about it," she admitted. "Easy way to jinx a good thing."

"I suggest you think about it, m'dear."

Ginna knew exactly what her friend meant. "There is no way I'd mention children to Zach. It's a perfect way to send a man running for the hills."

"Unless he's The One," Nora said slyly. "Then I doubt he'd run."

Ginna rolled her eyes. "I don't intend to test the theory."

"I thought you were over Denny when you faced him in court," Nora said.

"I was over him way before I filed for divorce. But I'm not sure I'm interested in getting married again."

"Liar," Nora accused. "You don't want to become so involved with a man that the subject of marriage will come up, because that will automatically lead to the subject of children."

Ginna flinched at her friend's direct statement, but Nora wasn't about to back down now.

"Just because Denny was a bastard doesn't mean that Zach would be. A majority of men who want to get married also want children, Ginna."

"Face it, Nora, I have it in writing that I can't have children. It was bad enough when we tried and I couldn't get pregnant. Then I'm thinking it's Denny. After all, he did have the mumps when he was in college. But to find out it's me? I come from a large family, with a history of large families."

"And has one member of your family said a thing

about this?'' Nora demanded. ''Have Brian or Mark or Jeff ever introduced you by saying, 'Hi, this is my barren sister?' How often has your mother insisted you're still a wonderful person and you can adopt?''

Ginna winced. ''Jeez, Nora, why don't you just cut one of my veins? No wonder you and Mark broke up.''

''Mark and I broke up because he made the mistake at that bar of ending up in a corner with that slutty fire-department groupie who was all over him,'' she said bluntly.

''Oh, yeah, that was the last time he tossed back a couple of boilermakers.'' Ginna sighed. ''I adore Zach, Nora. I think he is the most wonderful man to come along in a very long time. But I'm not going to risk my heart by falling in love with him.''

''Easier said than done.''

''HEY, GIN, WHEN YOU ASKED us to trim the bushes, you didn't say you wanted all of it done in one day,'' Mark Walker whined that afternoon as he studied the bushes lining the walkway to Ginna's front door.

''Yes, she did, lamebrain. You just refused to listen, as always.'' Jeff, eldest of the Walker brothers, opened a bottle of water and promptly swallowed half the contents.

''You know the deal. No work. No free haircuts,'' Ginna informed her brother Mark, who was still frowning at her.

''I have a date tonight,'' Mark said, running his hand through brown unruly locks.

Ginna picked up the pruning shears and handed them to him. ''Better get to work, then.''

''The lawn mower's low on gas,'' Brian said, checking the tank. "You still have some in the garage?" he asked his sister.

"Look at this. The guy gets married, becomes a dad and he's suddenly Mr. Responsibility in spades," Mark groused good-naturedly, pausing to strip off his T-shirt and toss it onto the steps. He realized his mistake when Casper growled and attacked the shirt. The dog picked it up with his teeth and whipped his head back and forth. Mark didn't bother trying to grab the shirt back. Not after the last time, when he'd lost the battle to the dog. And his favorite T-shirt.

"Great, Mark, get half-naked, so my female neighbors go nuts again," Ginna muttered, setting a cooler on the front steps. Past experience with her brothers taught her it was easier to keep cold drinks in a cooler outside than to have them tramping dirt on her carpet. While they worked hard as paramedics and firemen and were responsible in their work, they seemed to revert to their teenage years when they descended on her house.

She looked at her brothers. All tall, dark and handsome, with blue eyes that easily melted a woman's heart. She just saw them as pains in the butt who accused the family dogs of burying her Barbie dolls. Jeff and Brian might be married now, but it didn't stop other women from looking. Not that the men ever looked anywhere but at their wives.

Mark perked up as he looked around. "That cute little blonde still live two doors down?"

"Yes, she does. With her husband, the *professional wrestler,*" she said.

"Wrestlers are out. Paramedics are in." Mark flexed his muscles.

"Come on, Mark," Brian ordered. "Gail and I are taking the baby in for new pictures this afternoon."

Ginna mimed cracking a whip. "Get to work, or I'll call Mom," she threatened.

She smiled as her brothers immediately headed to their separate tasks.

"When do we meet your new guy?" Jeff asked.

"Never," she said promptly.

Brian pretended great interest in his sister as he walked around her.

"What are you doing?" she demanded.

"Looking for fingerprints. Maybe we need to get him checked out," he said to his brothers. "Make sure he doesn't have any deep dark secrets."

"He's absolutely normal, which is a wonderful change from you lunatics." Ginna gestured for Casper to follow her. "Remember, you have to go through the kitchen to get to the bathroom, not through the front door. I just had the carpet cleaned."

"You can cut my hair today, right?" Mark asked. "I've got a hot date tonight."

"I told you I'd do it, but I have an early dinner date, so I want you guys out of here by one."

"You're not having sex with this guy, are you?" Jeff asked, leaning on his rake. "And if you are, you're having safe sex, right?"

"*Jeff!*" Ginna felt the red steal up her throat and into her cheeks.

"Jeez, Jeff!" Brian and Mark yelled in unison.

"Do you think I want to think of my sister having sex?" Brian asked his brother.

"No more talk about sex!" Ginna shrieked. "I don't interfere in your lives. You don't interfere in mine. So help me, I hear one more word about Zach, I'm calling Mom. And then I'm calling Gail and Abby."

The three men grumbled their way back to their

chores. Ginna's threats were never made lightly. They applied themselves until she disappeared around the side of the house.

"I'll get his full name. You get someone to run it for a criminal record," Brian told his brothers.

ZACH WASN'T SURE what to do when he found the sidewalk in front of Ginna's house and her driveway crowded with two sport utility vehicles and a pickup truck. There was no missing the baby seats in the back of the two SUVs. Or the Firemen Are The Hottest sticker on the back bumper of the truck.

He rang the doorbell, positive he could hear laughter from the rear of the house. He refused to back down when Casper appeared at the screen door. Or when a muscular man appeared behind the dog.

"Hey there, you must be Zach," the man said, holding out his hand. "I'm Brian Walker, Ginna's brother. Come on back. I'm afraid she's running a little late. We do her yard work for her and she gives us free haircuts."

"Which goes to show who's getting the better deal here," Ginna called out. "Please tell me they swept the walkway."

"They swept the walkway," Zach said obediently, looking at three men who stared at him with a don't-mess-with-our-sister-or-we'll-have-to-hurt-you look. He didn't need to be told they were all related. All four shared the same brilliant blue eyes and brown hair.

"Jeff and Mark," Ginna said, gesturing to the man seated in a chair in front of her, then at the brother holding a bottle of water and leaning against the counter. "Don't let them say anything mean to you. Guys, this is Zach Stone."

Mark narrowed his gaze as he leaned forward and

shook Zach's hand. "You look familiar. Have we ever met?"

"He writes a magazine column," she explained. "Which lets you out, Mark, since we all know you prefer only magazines with pictures."

"She's always shown you her good side, hasn't she?" Jeff asked. "Enjoy it while it lasts. Suddenly one day she'll turn into this insane creature that belongs in a science-fiction movie."

"Her idea of threats involves calling our mom."

"Works every time," she said proudly, brandishing the hairdryer.

"Only because we were stupid enough to call her bluff one time," Brian told him.

"They were having water fights on my front lawn," Ginna explained. "They got Casper so excited he was howling. I thought my windows would shatter next. I told them if they didn't knock it off, I'd call Mom. They didn't. I did. She drove out here and set them straight."

"Our mother is small but mighty," Jeff explained. "What about you, Zach? Any family in the area?"

"Any insanity?" Mark muttered. "Ow!" He turned his head and glared at his sister. "There better not be any bruises."

"You should be so lucky."

"I have a sister and nephew who live in the area," Zach replied. "Our parents live back East."

"Okay, you're done," Ginna told her brother, taking away the towel that had covered his chest.

Mark stood up and hugged her. "Thanks, sis."

The other two men set their water bottles on the counter and paused long enough to give her a hug.

"Nice meeting you, Zach," Jeff said. "I just want to say if she shows any strange tendencies, don't worry.

They always go away after the full moon.'' He ducked as Ginna snapped a towel at his head.

"I've always been convinced they're adopted,'' she told Zach after her brothers had left.

"I tried that with my sister,'' he said. "Nobody believed me, either.''

"I'm sorry I'm running late. This was the only day they could do the yard work, and getting them over here at the same time is no less than a miracle. I'll be ready in no time. Help yourself to anything in the refrigerator.'' She started to leave the kitchen.

"Hey, wait a minute.'' Zach grabbed her hand and pulled her back to him. "Hello,'' he murmured, kissing her slowly.

She laughed softly and pressed herself against him, parting her lips to allow his tongue access.

A plaintive whine and paws batting at them finally convinced them to part.

"Give me ten minutes,'' Ginna said, moving away.

"I'll time you,'' he teased.

Zach sat down at the small oval wood table, surrounded by a wraparound bench, in the breakfast nook. Floor-to-ceiling windows overlooked the backyard. Freshly clipped grass and bright flowers met his gaze.

The house was warm and homey, the kitchen a room that looked well used, instead of just a place to store food. Judging from the rows of cookbooks lined up along white-painted shelves, she did a lot of cooking. The copper-bottomed pots and pans hanging from hooks overhead confirmed that assumption.

He noticed that a brightly colored pottery bowl with Casper's name painted on the side held kibble, while another bowl was filled with water. Both sat on a plastic

mat depicting a cartoon of a drooling dog looking upward in hungry anticipation.

The real-life dog sat in front of him, ever watchful.

"Her brothers told you to keep an eye on me, didn't
they?" he said to the dog.

He knew his kids would adore Casper. They'd be
ready to chase him and roll all over him. Trey had been
asking for a dog lately, but Zach had been putting him
off with the explanation they needed to wait awhile.
Then Emma asked for a kitten. He feared if he didn't
hold fast, he'd end up with a zoo. And if he kept feeling
this guilty about keeping Emma and Zach a secret, he'd
probably give in and buy them any pet they wanted.

"I bet you like kids," he said to the dog.

"Like them? He loves them." Ginna swept in looking
entirely different from the casually clad woman he'd
seen when he arrived.

While she had looked great in the denim cutoffs and
tank top she'd been wearing, she looked downright elegant and sexy in terra-cotta silk slacks and a matching
long blazer that remained open over a pale-peach top.
She'd pulled her hair up and back in an intricate twist.

"You are beautiful," he said honestly.

"Thank you." She beamed, spinning in a tight circle.
"And my sister-in-law thanks you. Jeff's wife, Abby,
makes just about all my clothes. I keep telling her she
could make a fortune doing this professionally. She
makes all her daughters' clothes. They have twin girls
and Abby likes to see them dressed alike but with in-
dividuality. I swear, she can look at an outfit in a magazine and copy it. Besides, I wanted us to match," she
teased, straightening his dark-coral-and-brown tie lying
neatly against a cream-colored shirt tucked into dark-
brown slacks.

"You weren't kidding when you said you're very close to your family," he said as they walked outside to his vehicle.

"We grew up in a pretty rural area," Ginna explained. "There were times we only had each other. My parents were very family-oriented, and I guess it seeped into us. But there are times when they're all a bit much. You're lucky you hadn't shown up an hour earlier. Those three get together and they suddenly revert back to their high-school days. Very sad." She shook her head in mock sympathy.

"They're right, you can be a scary woman."

"Be careful, Zachary." She leaned over to murmur in his ear. "The full moon starts tonight."

"Good thing I like to live dangerously."

THIS TIME ZACH CHOSE the beach. The restaurant was built on a cliff directly behind it. Tiki torches stationed in military order alongside the balcony and candles set on each table gave a romantic air. Ginna loved it all.

They sat on the balcony overlooking the beach so they could watch the surf come in as the sun set over the water. The breeze was cool, but they felt no desire to go inside just yet. The salty tang of the sea blended with the spice of Ginna's perfume.

Ginna fingered her wineglass. "There's something so relaxing about the water," she said idly. "Actually, I think it's just me and water. As long as there isn't a sailboard around." She smiled.

"Understandable." He sipped his scotch. "I'd finally decided those sailboards were designed to see just how much stress a person could take. I was beginning to see them as colorful firewood."

"Amazing, isn't it? All because we were given the

same seat on the plane," she mused. "What kind of fate factored into that?"

"Someone who pressed the wrong computer key," Zach guessed.

Ginna shook her head. "It's never that simple."

"It depends on who makes your reservations for you."

She made a face at him. "Come on, Zach, don't be so logical. Whether we like it or not, things happen for a reason."

He kept his eyes on her face. "A good reason, but sorry, I'm still voting for logic."

"It's not as much fun as waiting to see what will happen. To just do it," she argued playfully. "You went there for fun, didn't you? To relax?"

"My trip was a gift from my sister," he replied. "She decided it was time for me to take a vacation."

"And you didn't think you needed one?"

Zach shrugged. "I guess I never gave it a thought one way or another."

"Then you needed it. There're times when you need to get away from everyday life and think about just your-self for a short period of time," she said.

"Is that what you did?" he asked. "Go out there to think strictly about yourself?"

"In a way."

Zach looked out over the water that was turning a darker blue as the sun disappeared. "Because of that court case with your ex-husband?"

She could feel her smile slip off her lips. "A celebra-tion of sorts," she admitted. "A way of putting the past to rest. Total closure."

"Was it? Total closure, I mean?"

Ginna frowned, wondering where his questions were

going. "I have no feelings one way or another about my ex-husband," she said firmly. "We stopped being a couple three years ago. After it was over, he went his way and I went mine."

"But he hurt you," Zach said.

She started to say something, then snapped her mouth shut. She looked off as if she was searching for the right words.

"What he wanted wasn't possible," she said finally. "When he realized that, he went on to find exactly what he wanted."

"Then he definitely was a fool," Zach said quietly.

Ginna's smile held a hint of sorrow as she looked at him. "No, just a human being who couldn't handle unexpected surprises thrown his way."

JUST A HUMAN BEING who couldn't handle unexpected surprises thrown his way.

Ginna's quietly voiced statement haunted Zach as they sat inside for dinner. The sorrow in her eyes hadn't left right away, but she eventually bounced back into the cheerful Ginna he'd come to know. Still, he couldn't get her words out of his head as he ate his swordfish.

What kind of surprise would prompt a man to end a marriage? Especially a marriage to someone like Ginna? His forehead furrowed in a frown.

"You didn't have a sex-change operation or anything, did you?" he asked suddenly.

Ginna's head snapped up. Her laughter bubbled out. She set her water glass down.

"I have to say, that's a new one." She chuckled. "Is there a particular reason you would think that?" She wasn't insulted as much as intrigued by his query.

"Strong family resemblance." He was privately relieved he could at least come up with a reason that made some sense.

She nodded. "If my idiot brothers tried to make you believe I was once a man, I will happily kill them. Actually, we all look alike. My younger sister could be my twin. I only have to look at my mother to know what I'll look like in about twenty-five years. I must say I am going to look fantastic." She grinned. "What do you think you and your wife would have contributed to the family gene pool?" Ginna asked.

"I think we would have created a couple of great kids." He didn't miss her deft way of changing the subject.

She fingered her glass, sliding a forefinger around the rim. "It must have been hard. Losing her so early in your marriage," she murmured.

Zach nodded. "Not exactly what I expected. For a long time I blamed her for leaving me."

She nodded, understanding the reason for his words. "I've heard when a spouse dies that it's natural to feel anger."

"I wasn't just angry that she was taken from me. I was angry that she was taken so soon. She was too young to die," he said. "It was one of those freak things that no one plans for. I eventually put my grief to one side and tried to go on with my life." His smile was that of a sorrow long laid to rest.

"She must have been a special lady," Ginna murmured.

"That she was." He smiled at her. "You would have liked each other."

"I'm sure we would have," she agreed. "And I have an idea it wouldn't be just because we have the same taste in men." She smiled, then returned to discussing a less painful topic. "What about you and your sister? Who do each of you resemble?"

"Lucie took after our dad and I took after our mom. Of course, it also has to do with her having her hair colored and wearing colored contact lenses."

"Don't blame that on the estrogen crowd," she protested. "I have some male clients who have highlights added to their hair." She narrowed her gaze as she studied him.

He held up his hands in protest. "No. Don't even think it."

Ginna's eyes danced. "Gotcha."

He chuckled. "Talk about a major scare."

"It's fallout from spending part of the day with my brothers. The effects should wear off soon." She stole a bit of his swordfish, then thoughtfully placed a piece of her mahi mahi on his plate. "There're days when they act worse than their kids. Actually, the kids tend to act older than them."

"Maybe you need to add to the family gene pool. Show them how to do it right." He made it a light comment, but the fleeting darkness in her eyes surprised him.

"My sisters-in-law do more than their share," she replied, suddenly focusing all her attention on her food.

Another puzzle, Zach thought. Ginna seemed genuinely fond of her family, but he'd swear something also kept her separate from them.

Now he just had to solve the puzzle and put everything together.

After dinner, they went into the bar, which boasted a dance floor. He saw it as a good excuse to have her in his arms.

They both chose coffee over an after-dinner drink and spent most of their time on the dance floor. It was so crowded they could only move in small steps, but that was fine with them.

"Zach?" Her breath was warm in his ear.

"Hm?".

"Stay with me tonight."

Chapter Nine

Zach wasn't sure what he expected to find in Ginna's bedroom, but an oasis wasn't it.

Lamps on either side of the large bed emitted a pleasant glow over a lilac-print comforter that Ginna was in the process of turning back.

She'd discarded her shoes and blazer. Her pale-peach top glowed against her lightly tanned skin.

She looked over her shoulder and smiled.

Guilt about the kids was hanging over his head. Lucie had been only too happy to keep them for the night when he'd gone off to call her and muttered the request. She teased him to be good and not worry about the kids.

Looking at the seductive vision of Ginna plumping up the pillows put everything else out of his mind.

"Okay, handsome," she said, walking over to him. She slid her fingers down his neck and loosened his tie, sliding it down his front and tossing it over her shoulder. She pulled his shirt out of his slacks, then neatly undid each button. She ran her hands across his now-bare chest. "Nice," she murmured, touching his nipple with her tongue.

Zach jumped as if she'd touched him with a live wire.

"Damn, Ginna!" he gasped, grabbing hold of her arms.

"That good, huh?" She gently nibbled the copper-colored disk. "I've been thinking about doing this all evening."

"I've been having more than a few thoughts of my own. Starting with this." He grasped the hem of her top and pulled it over her head. He muttered a few words of praise when he revealed a peach-toned lace bra.

"Everything matches," she informed him.

"I can't wait to find that out for myself." He reached for the waistband of her pants, but she stepped back. She unzipped and unbuttoned, then slid the pants down her legs.

Zach was convinced his heart stopped when he stared at her. She was wearing not only lacy bikini panties that matched her bra, but also sheer thigh-high stockings with lacy tops.

His pants were quickly tossed to one side as he made his way over to her. She smiled broadly as she walked backward in time to his forward advance. She stopped when the back of her knees hit the side of the bed.

"Did I ever tell you that I think your boxers are very sexy?" she asked, tracing the waistband as she sat on the bed.

"No, but please feel free to do so."

She continued running the tip of her nail around the skin just above the waistband. "They hint at what's beneath without giving anything away." Now she started to trace the front, which was taut. "And oh-so-happy to see me." Without further ado, she grasped the waistband and pulled him down onto the bed beside her. "Aha! I have you now, my pretty," she cackled.

"Correction." He grabbed her arms and shifted until

she lay under him. "*I've* got *you*." He lowered his head and captured her mouth in a kiss meant to swamp her senses.

As their tongues tangled, Zach released the catch to her bra and slipped the garment off.

"Just couldn't resist stripping me, could you?" she teased.

"Be good and I'll let you keep the stockings on." He ran a hand up her silky calf. "Come to think of it, you can be as bad as you like, and I'll still let you keep the stockings on."

"What a gentleman." She lifted a leg to run her silk-covered toes along his hip.

Zach then proceeded to show Ginna just what kind of gentleman he was.

Every word he uttered was dark with a sensuality that shook Ginna to her core. Not to be outdone, she matched him word for word, saying what she intended to do to him. What she wanted him to do to her.

"Anything to please a lady," he said as he rested his hand against the hollow below her navel. Then he moved lower, tangling his fingers in the soft curls that hid her core. He smiled as he felt how damp she was. He moved his fingers inward. She arched up under his touch. "I want you to burn for me, Ginna," he urged her in a low throbbing voice.

"I'm already doing that!" She twisted and turned under his touch.

He found the ultrasensitive spot and pressed down lightly.

"*Zach!*" she cried, trying to grab hold of his hand. He grasped her wrist and held it off to the side.

"It's only going to get better," he promised, dropping a kiss on her lips.

Her eyes were glazed with desire as she looked up at him. "Anything better on my part will only kill you." Her threat was ignored as he continued trailing kisses along her collarbone while his fingers worked their magic.

Except Ginna found a way to extract some revenge of her own.

"As I said, boxers hold such delightful things." Her smile was pure sin.

After that, it was Zach who was eager to move things along.

GINNA HAD the perfect bed.

One that wasn't so feminine it scared off a man.

The kind of bed any man wouldn't mind sharing with the right woman.

Enough room for a guy to spread out, and also comfortable for cuddling.

If it wasn't for the extremely large dog boldly making his way straight down the middle.

Once Casper reached the head of the bed, he rolled over onto his side with his paws placed firmly against Zach. And pushed.

Zach, who'd been sleeping, was abruptly awakened as he landed hard on the floor.

"What happened?" Ginna sat up in bed.

Zach sat up, too, and glared at the dog, who was the picture of innocence.

"Your dog pushed me out of bed. Deliberately."

"Deliberately?" She giggled. "No, it's just that he normally sleeps up here. Casper, bad boy," she scolded. The dog appeared to hang his head in shame. "Back on the floor. Now," she ordered.

Casper slowly rose to his feet and slunk off the bed. But not without shooting Zach an it's-all-your-fault look.

Zach winced as he climbed back into bed. Ginna moved into the warm circle of his arms. She planted a kiss on his shoulder.

"I'm glad you're here," she said just before she fell back to sleep.

Zach was starting to drift off when he felt a shifting along the end of the bed. He opened his eyes and watched the dog-shaped shadow stretch out across the foot. He was positive the dog gave a silent snarl before settling down.

"No way I'll let you win the battle," he whispered to the dog.

But as he fell back to sleep, he was positive Casper was laughing at him.

"WHAT, YOU DIDN'T THINK I could cook?" Ginna asked as she placed a plate loaded with pancakes, sausages and eggs in front of Zach the next morning. Aromatic coffee and a wineglass filled with orange juice finished the meal.

"More like you're trying to kill me with food." He picked up a fork, not knowing where to start.

Ginna shook her head. She shifted sideways and slid onto his lap. She reached for her fork and used it to cut off a section of pancake, which she lifted to his mouth.

"Guaranteed to build up your strength. Buttermilk pancakes," she cooed, waving it in front of his mouth. "With rich cinnamon syrup."

He obediently opened his mouth and closed it over the fork. Chewed.

She looked at him expectantly.

"Damn, that's good," he said after swallowing. He angled his arms around her and cut off another piece.

"Of course it is," she said, no doubt at all.

She got up off his lap and fixed a plate for herself. She sat down next to him, her hip bumping companionably against his. She glanced outside, where Casper was patrolling the yard. Every once in a while he looked up at the fence, then resumed his march. "A neighbor's cat likes to sit on the fence and tease him. He's convinced the day will come when he'll get that cat."

"I'm rooting for the cat."

She shook her head at him. "Be nice. I expect the two males in my life to get along."

"Yeah, well, I think your dog has a different idea on how to get along." He continued eating.

Within minutes of waking up, they had been involved in doing a lot more than greeting each other with "Good morning." Zach was still reeling from Ginna's idea of how to start the day.

After her shower, she'd donned a cream-colored eyelet robe that tied at the waist with a pale blue sash. It had a nice habit of parting every so often to show off her legs. She'd done something to her hair that left it in waves. Her face was bare of makeup, and all she wore on her feet was a coat of spice-colored toenail polish.

It had been a long time since he'd shared breakfast with a woman. Even then, it had been nothing like this particular breakfast.

This one was leisurely, filled with quiet conversation. He didn't need to coax Emma to eat her cereal while threatening Trey with no games for a week if he dared to put any more banana in his own cereal. No demands for more milk or juice. No refereeing battles over who got the Rugrats bowl since its mate was broken.

This morning it was up to Lucie to handle those matters.

He loved his kids with all his heart, but sometimes it was nice to have an entirely adult meal.

Ginna offered Zach his choice of which part of the newspaper he would like to read. He declined, since he preferred talking to her.

"What magic do you spin around a man?" he asked after he'd finished his second helping of pancakes. "My idea of breakfast is maybe a bowl of cereal if I'm lucky."

"You think I eat like this all the time?" she asked with amusement. "Consider this a treat for you. My favorite meal is breakfast, and if I have the time, I like to fix something special like pancakes or French toast, but if I want something like that, it's usually easier to go out. There're a lot of mornings when I'm running out the door with an energy bar in one hand and a cup of coffee in the other so I won't be late for my first appointment." She dropped a kiss on his head as she walked past him.

He glanced at the clock and felt instant guilt. He never stayed out this late without calling in. It was bad enough his sister figured out what he was doing all night.

And would demand details.

Of which she would get none.

"You need to go soon, don't you." Ginna easily read his mind.

He hoped he didn't look as guilty as he felt.

"I have some things I need to do," he started to explain.

She shook her head and placed her fingertips against his lips to silence him.

"I asked you to stay with me last night," she said

softly. "Having that was special. Don't think you have to spend the day with me or feel the need to make explanations because you can't."

"I'll help with the dishes," he offered.

"You can dry."

He needed to tell her about Emma and Trey. He could have found a way while they did the breakfast dishes, but the time didn't seem right.

She'll think you're ashamed of your kids when that's not it at all. All this time together and you never mentioned them.

Maybe if he could get her to talk about her nieces and nephews again. He'd been racking his brain for just the right comment when her phone rang. It was her sister-in-law calling to ask if Ginna could look after her twin nieces that afternoon since Cathy Walker was unavailable.

"I'll be there," she promised, then hung up. "Did you know little girls scream loud enough to shatter glass?" she said. "My nieces have a decibel range that could deafen a person. My mother loves it. She would have taken them in a second, but she has her kickboxing class this afternoon."

Maybe it wasn't the time to bring up Emma and Trey, after all.

EMMA HOPPED into her father's arms.

"Nick made really gross noises last night," she informed him. "He said a troll got inside him and made him make the noises."

"I bet your aunt Lucie really loved that," Zach chuckled.

"More like Aunt Lucie grounded her darling son for the next week," Lucie told him, walking into the family room. "Why is it that when I punish him, I have to punish myself at the same time?"

"Same thing when school suspends him. They call it punishment for him being out of school. He calls it fantastic."

"See what Aunt Lucie did to my hair?" Emma twirled in a circle.

Zach dutifully admired the intricate braid. "It's very pretty."

"If I had a mom, I bet she could make my hair this pretty every day," she announced with a sly look at her dad.

"I think I do a pretty good job with your hair." He pretended hurt.

"But you're not a mom," Emma pointed out.

Lucie sat on the arm of the couch. She grinned broadly at her brother's discomfort. "Gee, Zach, all you'd have to do is find someone who can do hair," she said innocently. "I can't imagine it would be that difficult."

He shot her a frown that implied she not help. Her smile told him she wasn't about to stop now.

"And Aunt Lucie let me put on her lipstick," Emma chattered.

"A tinted lip balm," she clarified.

"And she gave me makeup!" Emma said with girlish glee as she thrust out her hands, which sported pink nails. "And she painted my nails, too. Aren't they pretty?"

Zach stared at his sister.

"The Pretty Belle makeup kit for little girls," she explained. She smiled at Emma. "Sweetie, why don't you go see what Trey and Nick are doing?"

"Terrific. My daughter isn't even out of preschool and

already she's wearing makeup," he whispered furiously after Emma left the room.

"Don't worry, I didn't let her call any boys and I locked her in the bedroom so she couldn't sneak out of the house to party," Lucie replied, unaffected by his anger.

"Luce, she's only four." He felt his life spiraling out of control.

"She's a four-year-old girl who wants a mother. As she gets older, that feeling will grow stronger," she told him.

"If it's such a natural feeling, why haven't you gone hunting for a dad for Nick?" he grumbled. "I'm sure there's a corrections officer out there who might think you're hot stuff."

"Thank you so much!" She threw a pillow at him. "Maybe I should advertise in one of those mercenary magazines," she said with a sarcastic bite.

Zach thought about it. "Might work." He ducked as another pillow hit his head.

"Enough about me. What about you and your new lady? I want to hear about your date. You must really like her."

He mentally ran through his evening. Safe enough to talk about.

And the rest of the night that followed. *Not one word.*

"She's special," he said finally, opting for what was safe dialogue.

Lucie arched an eyebrow. "Special? Gee, there has to be more to her than just saying she's special, although that is a sweet thing to say. And?" she prompted.

"And I like her a lot." *What an understatement!*

She rolled her eyes. "Like her a lot? That's what you say about your mechanic, Zach, not what you say about a woman you're dating. Special was good. Expand on that.''

"Why can't we talk about your dates?'' he growled, shifting uneasily.

"I'll tell you what. If I ever get lucky enough to have a date again, I'll let you interrogate me. Considering I haven't had one in over a year, I wouldn't advise you to hold your breath.'' She met his gaze directly. "Why don't we get down to the nitty-gritty here? Have you told her about Emma and Trey yet?''

He shook his head.

Lucie grimaced. "You need to tell her,'' she said softly.

"You're not telling me anything I haven't told myself,'' he said. "It's not as if I can say 'By the way, I have four-year-old twins,' while we're having our morning coffee.''

When he lifted his head, he noticed a strange expression cross his sister's face.

"What's wrong, Luce?'' he asked.

She hesitated, then smiled and shook her head. "It's nothing. Maybe overload. I just finished setting up a tour for fifteen seventy-year-old ladies who plan to whoop it up across Europe. They each had something different in mind, and I had to find a way to give them all what they wanted. By the time I finished, I was ready for a nervous breakdown. Except I had to pick up Nick from school and take him to tae kwon do class.''

Zach felt instant guilt. "I'm sorry, sis. I should be giving you a break, instead of loading up your life. What if I take Nick for you next weekend? Give you a chance to have some time to yourself.''

"So I could do what? Enjoy the silence?''

"Then take some time for yourself the way you told

me to take some for myself,'' he urged her. ''What about that spa you like to go to?'' He noticed a wave of color cross her face. ''See? You're not thinking it's so bad, after all.''

''Then you've got it, big brother. I'm taking you up on your offer. Nick is all yours. I'll set up appointments for a manicure, pedicure, facial and massage,'' she told him. ''Then I'll call a few friends and see if we can do a girls' night out.''

''Just tell Nick he can't talk Trey into trying to take over the country on my watch.''

Lucie got up and walked over to Zach. She hugged him tightly.

''You're my favorite brother, you know,'' she murmured, kissing his cheek.

''I'm your *only* brother.''

''Yes, but I love you, anyway.'' She hugged him again. ''I want you to be happy, Zach. You deserve the best.''

''I intend to tell her, Luce,'' he said. ''Soon.''

''Do it the easy way. Take Nick with you. She'll be so grateful he's not your son that she'll instantly adore Emma and Trey.''

''See my lipstick, Daddy!'' Emma ran into the room with a slash of red across her mouth.

Zach muttered a curse.

''Emma, that isn't the lip balm I gave you,'' Lucie said, peering closer at her niece's face. She winced at the vivid color.

''Nick told me I could have it,'' Emma said, wide-eyed.

''Oh, damn.'' Zach examined his daughter's face, then looked up at his sister. Frustration warred with anger. ''This was done with a marking pen.'' He swiveled around and bellowed, ''Nick!'' at the same time his sister did.

ZACH SOON LEARNED no amount of scrubbing could erase the color on Emma's lips. He'd ended up slathering some ointment on her chapped lips before putting her to bed.

''I guess I should be grateful he colored within the lines,'' he muttered, dropping onto his bed.

Nick hadn't seen the error of his ways. His defense was that he was helping Emma with her makeup. He heard his mother complain her lipstick didn't stay on the way she wanted it to. He just made sure Emma's would stay on.

A smile reluctantly tugged at the corners of his mouth.

The young boy had been so solemn when he explained what he'd done and why he didn't feel he should be punished.

''Daddy?''

He looked up and found Emma standing in the doorway.

''What's wrong, Peanut?''

Taking his question as an invitation to enter, she ran into the bedroom and leaped onto the bed. She bounced on her knees next to him.

He winced as he looked at her reddened mouth.

Emma continued bouncing until he grasped her hand in a silent entreaty to stop.

''You want to make Daddy seasick?'' he asked.

She giggled. ''You don't get seasick.''

''But I could. What's wrong?''

''Nothin'.'' Unable to remain still, she didn't bounce but moved restlessly. ''Don't be mad at Nick, Daddy.''

"Think how long we spent trying to get that marker off," he told her.

"I told him I wanted to look pretty so you could find me and Trey a mommy," she told him.

Zach felt as if he'd been punched in the stomach. One look at her tiny face told him just how serious she was.

"Peanut, you don't need makeup to look pretty. You are already the best-looking girl around," he said sincerely. "But you're doing it again. You're making me feel unloved." He pretended to pout.

She giggled and launched herself into his arms. She pursed her lips and gave him a smacking kiss on the nose. "I love you, Daddy, but I need a mommy. When Trey grows up, he'll need a daddy more, but I'm a girl. I need a mommy for mommy things," she explained.

"We've got Aunt Lucie," he pointed out. He could easily visualize a good mommy figure. Although the woman in question didn't even know he was a father.

"Daddy!" She harrumphed at him, her hands planted on her skinny hips.

Guilt took over as he realized he hadn't been listening.

"I'm sorry, baby. What did you say?"

"I said—" she gave a heaving sigh "—please look for a nice mommy for us. And don't waste any time." She wagged her finger at him.

It took all of his self-control not to laugh at her perfect imitation of her aunt Lucie. He knew if he did, his daughter would really let him have it.

"I will do whatever is necessary," he said seriously.

Emma looked suspicious. "You mean it?"

"I mean it." He kissed her on the forehead. "Come on, back to bed for my favorite girl."

"Don't worry, Daddy, I know you won't give us a mean mommy," she assured him after he tucked her in.

Zach looked at her nestled under her ruffled bedcovers. His little princess ensconced in her castle.

He placed his hand over his heart. "I promise I will not give you an evil queen who will send you out into the cold dark forest where you'll be rescued by seven trolls who all look like Nick."

Emma's giggle grew louder.

"Good night, my princess," he murmured, walking out and making sure the door was open its requisite five inches. "Sweet dreams."

He returned to his bedroom and picked up the book he'd planned to read that evening. The fast-paced plot couldn't hold his interest.

Emma was talking more and more about having a mother. He was grateful for Lucie stepping in when necessary. She'd been a godsend in helping out when something cropped up that Zach couldn't do. He was more than willing to take cupcakes to preschool for special occasions and help out as a chaperon when the students took a field trip. He'd enjoyed himself until a couple of single mothers took too personal an interest in him.

"Robby's mom is nice," Trey once told him, "but she smells really weird." He wrinkled his nose. "Her perfume makes me sneeze and she hugs me too much."

Emma was more honest.

"Robby's mommy only likes to go shopping and make herself pretty. And Robby's nanny isn't very nice," she confided.

Zach stayed out of Robby's mom's way after that. Luckily Robby's mom soon married a financial consultant who could afford her hobby of shopping.

Zach couldn't believe he was thinking marriage. It wasn't something he'd considered doing a second time. He didn't see the need for a wife. He was a pretty well-rounded dad, willing to do whatever was necessary for his kids.

But lately, he wasn't thinking about marrying just for the children. He wanted to do it for himself, as well.

He'd liked those nights he spent with Ginna. Not just the sex, but the cuddling, the conversation.

Ginna never lacked for conversation.

He never considered himself someone who thought in terms of hearts and flowers, but it was easy to think that way where she was concerned.

Personality of sunshine. Smile that made a guy just feel damn good.

And a pair of legs that had him feeling some even better thoughts.

It was way past time for him to tell Ginna about Emma and Trey. Especially since he also had to tell her he was falling in love with her.

Chapter Ten

"I really appreciate your taking me on such short notice, Gin," Lucie said, trying not to fidget in the chair. "At first, I was going to wallow in having time to myself, then I decided I'd rather wallow in some pampering."

"No problem. I had a light schedule for a Saturday," she said, wielding the hairdryer like a weapon. "Pampering oneself is always a good idea. I have to say, and not just because it's my handiwork, but these new highlights are going to look awesome."

"When I was growing up I was a towhead. Then as I got older, my hair kept getting darker while my brother's hair stayed blond," she said, watching the transformation take place. She smiled at her reflection. "Wow."

"Uh-huh." Ginna ran her fingers through the short blond curls. "You needed a change and, m'dear, you got it." She pulled off the drape. "You really went for the works today."

"My brother was going to take Nick for the weekend. Then the parents of one of Nick's friends called and asked if Nick could go to Disneyland with them for the weekend. Dear uncle was immediately forgotten." She chuckled. "I had time to myself. I wasted no time book-ing appointments for a body wrap, manicure and pedicure and a facial. Now this. I walked in early this morning feeling so drab and now I feel gorgeous." She happily wrote out a check. "If this new me doesn't catch a man, I am totally hopeless."

"Hopeless you're not," Ginna said, adjusting an errant curl. She glanced at a note the receptionist had dropped off for her.

Zach's coming in for a haircut? she thought. She'd trimmed his hair barely a week ago.

She smiled.

"You look way too happy," Lucie told her with a knowing glint in her eye.

"I am," she admitted.

Lucie stood up and hugged her. "At least someone I know is having fun with a man."

"Aunt Lucie!" A small body launched itself into her arms.

"Emma." Lucie seemed stunned as she looked down at her niece, then over at her brother.

"You look so pretty! Daddy said I can have a grown-up haircut." The little girl looked from Lucie to Ginna. "Hi," she said brightly, offering her a big grin.

"Hi," Ginna said slowly, her gaze swiveling from Emma to Lucie to the man standing off to one side with a small boy standing next to him.

Zach.

Lucie uttered a soft groan. "This is not how you do it, big brother."

"Brother?" Ginna's eyes widened.

Looking at them standing together, she could see the resemblance. Now she understood why she sometimes thought Zach looked familiar. At the moment she couldn't look at him. She turned to the little girl Lucie had just lowered to the floor. She'd called Lucie Aunt, which meant Zach was her father, which meant…

"Hi, Zach," Nora greeted him, quickly stepping through the thick wall of silence between the three adults. "If your daughter is getting a grown-up haircut, what about your big guy getting one, too? It doesn't seem fair that he doesn't get one."

"I'm Zachary Michael Stone III," the boy announced proudly.

Nora grinned. "A big name for a big guy."

"That's why Daddy named me Trey," he explained.

"Well, Trey—" Nora hunkered down to his level "—Ginna's great at giving girls grown-up haircuts, but I'm even better when it comes to guys. Think you're willing to let me give you a big-guy haircut?"

Trey looked up at Zach, who nodded.

"My treat," she told Zach in a low voice. "Besides, I think you're going to have to worry more about losing several layers of skin when she cuts your hair next time." She held out her hand and Trey took it without hesitation.

"So, Emma." Ginna dredged up a smile as she crouched down in front of the little girl. She noticed the girl's lips were a little too red. Past experience told her the girl had substituted a permanent marker for lipstick. "I'd say you're ready for a grown-up haircut. Do you have an idea what you'd like me to do with your hair? We have some books that show girl's haircuts. Do you want to look through them for ideas?"

Zach started to step forward, then froze when Ginna's glacial glare hit him full force.

"Why don't you wait in the reception area while I cut Emma's hair?" she suggested in a deceptively soft voice.

Instead of handing Emma over to a shampoo girl, Ginna took her back herself. She used the special strawberry-scented conditioning shampoo the salon kept for their younger clients. Emma declared it "neat."

"What made you decide it was time for a grown-up haircut?" Ginna asked her.

Emma waved her hands in the air. "I'm going to kindergarten in the fall," she confided. "I can't have a little-girl haircut for kindergarten, can I?"

Ginna hid her smile. "No, you can't," she replied seriously. "I can understand why you feel this is so important."

"Daddy says you cut his hair. Do you cut Aunt Lucie's hair, too?"

"Yes, I do. Do you like what I did with her hair today?"

"It's very pretty." Emma wiggled in the chair. "Aunt Lucie doesn't have a boyfriend," she whispered. "Prob'ly 'cause of Nick. He's my cousin. Daddy says he'll either end up in politics or in prison."

"I have three brothers and they're all like that," Ginna told her. "But they grew up okay."

"He's sitting out there looking about as miserable as a man can look," Nora murmured as she set Trey up at the next shampoo bowl.

"The man is dead meat," she said in a low voice while keeping a bright smile on her lips.

"I cannot wait to hear this story," Nora said before turning to Trey. "Okay, big guy, let's get started with a shampoo." She laughed when the boy made a face. "Hey, at least you're not getting a bath!"

"I don't need a bath," Trey told her. "I had one last night."

As Ginna escorted Emma back to her station, she

looked toward the reception area. Zach sat on the couch where he would see them.

Nora was right—he did look miserable. Lucie sat next to him with a tense expression on her face. She was turned sideways talking intently to Zach.

Good, let him suffer big time, she thought maliciously as she set a booster seat in her chair for Emma, then draped her in a plastic cape.

She smiled and talked to the little girl, while a dozen questions ran through her mind. Not that she had any answers to them.

Why hadn't he told her he had children? What was the big secret about them?

She put her thoughts on hold as she showed Emma a book of children's hairstyles. After careful deliberation, they chose a short style that would suit Emma's elfin features.

"If you have your hair that short, you won't be able to wear a ponytail or a braid," Ginna warned before she made the first snip. "Are you okay with that?"

Emma didn't hesitate. She nodded. "That's okay. Then Daddy won't have as much to comb in the morning. He says I get a lot of tangles."

"Okay." Ginna began snipping.

As she combed and clipped, Emma kept up a running conversation, jumping from one subject to another, starting with her brother, then telling her about her school, her desire for a puppy or a kitten and her cousin's antics.

Lucie had talked about her son during her appointments, but it was through Emma that Ginna heard stories she swore would have turned her own parents' hair gray.

"You're very pretty," Emma said when Ginna finished. She looked up with brown eyes just like her father's. "Do you have a boyfriend? Would you like to go out with my dad? He's really nice. You cut his hair, so maybe you already know how nice he is.''

Ginna was speechless. Obviously Emma didn't know about their dating.

"Maybe Ginna would like to go out for pizza with us," Zach said, walking up to them. He reached over for Emma and lifted her out of the seat. "You look gorgeous, Peanut. You're a regular grown-up now."

Emma beamed with pleasure.

"Hey me!" Trey insisted on his own share of praise.

Zach grinned and shook his head. "Definitely on your way to the big leagues," he told his son. He reached into his back pocket.

"If you dare try to pay me, I will cut off your hand," Ginna said for his ears only. "And then I will cut off something else." Her eyes drifted south for a brief second. Just long enough to make her point known.

He quickly backed off.

"So you'll have pizza with us?" Emma asked, tugging on Ginna's hand. "Please?"

"Ginna, please?" Zach added his own plea.

When she turned to him, she noticed Lucie standing behind him, mouthing, *Go!*

"I just need to clean my station," she said.

"We'll wait over there." Zach shot her a silent thank-you and urged the twins over to the couch.

"Lucie." Ginna's softly spoken word stopped the woman.

"Time to go," Lucie said cheerfully.

"You knew I was dating your brother." Ginna gathered up her brushes.

"Yes."

"Yet you never told me."

"I didn't want things to be awkward. Look, it's my

fault," she went on hurriedly. "When Zach was taking the trip, I told him to be selfish for once in his life. To be Zach, the man. Not Zach, the father. To give him the opportunity to be himself for a while. Then he didn't know how to tell you about the twins. I think he's already figured out just bringing them in here was not a good idea. If you'd rather talk to him privately, I'll take the twins."

Ginna's stomach tightened. "No, they're looking forward to this. Besides, I need to do this," she said more to herself.

"I'm sorry." Lucie looked upset.

"No, don't be." Ginna managed a smile. "It had to happen sooner or later. It may as well be now."

Lucie nodded jerkily and made her escape.

Ginna went into the rear of the salon where she could take a few minutes to compose herself.

For a moment, tears threatened to fall.

He has children.

And here she'd intimated that children weren't something she wanted in her life. He never said a word.

She felt like throwing up.

It took a few moments for her hand to stop shaking before she touched up her eyeshadow and lipstick.

"Look at it this way. He has kids. That takes the pressure off you." Nora stood in the doorway. She shrugged. "All right, not exactly tactful, but I don't think you want to hear any tact right now."

Ginna's retort was less than ladylike. Nora arched an eyebrow.

"I guess that didn't make it better for you."

"No," Ginna snapped. Then she shook her head. "I'm sorry. You're trying to make me feel better in your usual no-nonsense way and I'm ready to bite your head off.''

''When the head you really want to bite off is Zach's,'' Nora finished for her. ''Trey thinks you're cuter than Robby's mom. From what he said about the woman, I'd say that's a good thing. Don't keep the guy feeling too miserable, okay?''

''I'll think about it.'' Ginna dropped the lipstick into her cosmetic case and zipped it shut.

When she walked out to the reception area, she was smiling at the trio waiting for her.

''I'll warn you now. No anchovies,'' she declared.

''Yuck!'' Emma wrinkled her nose.

''Mushrooms are yucky too,'' Trey told her as they walked outside.

''They're better than those little fishes,'' she said. She looked down when she found a small hand tucked inside hers. Emma looked up with a broad smile. Ginna couldn't help but smile back.

''We're going to one of those pizza places where the games are more popular than the food,'' Zach warned. ''The kids love it there.''

''Nothing new to me. I've gone there before and survived.''

''I know we need to talk,'' he murmured.

Her gaze sliced through him like a laser.

''Oh, we will.''

ZACH WAS FINDING OUT what true misery was. And it wasn't any fun.

It started out that afternoon with Emma insisting she had to have a grown-up haircut and why couldn't she go where he went. He now knew he was stupid. He thought if he took the twins to where Ginna worked, she would meet them, see how special they were and so on. Which he knew she did.

His ears still smarted from Lucie's lecture.

"I told you to tell her about the twins. Not rub them in her face!" she practically spat out the words as she kept her voice low so they wouldn't be overheard.

"What was I supposed to do? Emma got it in her head today that she wanted a grown-up haircut," he muttered. "I told her I'd call Tia to see if she could fit her in. Emma argues that Tia cuts little girls' hair. She wanted to go where I go."

Lucie shook her head, muttering about idiotic fathers who give in to their daughters. "You tell her Tia cuts her hair and Ginna cuts yours. You tell her Ginna couldn't fit her in."

"That's lying," he protested.

"And what have you been doing to Ginna?"

"Who told me to go to Hawaii and just be Zach, the man, not Zach, the dad?" he countered.

"Lovely, blame it on me. It doesn't work that way, Zach." She leaned forward and lowered her voice. "I'd like to remind you that you've had plenty of opportunities to tell her the truth. Are you in love with her?"

He took a deep breath. Tension tightened his features. "Not exactly a good place to discuss this, Luce."

She spared a quick glance toward the back of the salon. Ginna still hadn't reappeared. Lucie picked up her purse and looped the strap over her shoulder as she stood up.

"All right, I'll take partial responsibility because I did tell you to go there as some swinging bachelor. Which it seems you did a great job of portraying," she said. "I'm out of here." She headed for the door.

"Luce?"

She stopped and looked over her shoulder.

Suddenly something occurred to Zach that he desperately needed to know the answer to.

"Did you book Ginna's trip, too?"

"I book a lot of trips, Zach," was all she said as she pushed open the door and left. "It is what I do for a living."

Suspicion reared its ugly head as he watched his sister walk down the sidewalk.

Apparently Lucie was even more devious than he thought.

THE PIZZA PLACE was everything it advertised. And more.

Bright lights, lots of noise, games of every description for a child and those with an inner child.

Emma and Trey were happy bouncing around in a room filled with multicolored plastic balls while Ginna and Zach sat at a bright purple table with even brighter red-painted chairs. Ginna wore an ankle-length dress patterned with swirls of reds, oranges, golds, purples and midnight blue.

Zach couldn't take his eyes off her.

"I should have told you about the twins before now. I'm an idiot and I will do whatever is necessary to get back in your good graces," he said slowly. "If I'd had any sense, I wouldn't have listened to Lucie. I should have known better, since her past advice hasn't always been the best."

She was intrigued. "Such as?"

"I'd have to go back to high school, and it wouldn't be a pretty sight." He picked up his slice of pizza and munched on it. "Did Lucie book your trip?"

"Of course." Ginna was surprised by his question.

"When I told her I won my case and that I wanted to take a trip, she said she would handle everything for me."

"Which, I have a sneaking suspicion, has to do with our somehow ending up with the same seat assignment," he said softly.

Her expression changed as his words sunk in. "Wait a minute."

Zach nodded. "Exactly."

"Are you saying that Lucie set us up?"

"With Lucie, anything is possible. She's been nagging me to date more," he admitted. "She booked both our trips and we end up not only on the same flight, but the same seat. What does that say?"

"She thought I was depressed about seeing my ex-husband again," she mused. "When all I really wanted to do was never see him again in this lifetime. So she decided to get us together."

"Yep." Zach looked at her hopefully. "Does this mean you're no longer mad at me?"

"Oh, I'm mad," Ginna replied in her soft lethal voice. Along with the anger sparking her eyes was a hint of sorrow, a sorrow that tore at Zach's heart. "I can't easily forgive you for what you kept from me. I think of all those times I talked about my nieces and nephew and yet you never said one damn word." She shook her head. "It hurts, Zach. You're lucky I don't hold grudges." She paused. The intensity in her voice didn't change, but the timbre did, sending chills up and down his spine as she said, "Can you imagine what a couple of inventive adults could do in that enclosure with all those plastic balls?"

Zach gulped.

She kept her voice low so they couldn't be overheard

as she told him just what she was thinking. After that, she moved on to a few other of the play areas in the restaurant. By the time she finished, Zach's slice of pizza hung limply from his hand.

"Oh, you are good," he said once he recovered his vocal chords.

She smiled. "A good thing to remember."

"You're not done torturing me, are you."

"Oh, Zach, you don't know what torture is." She presented him with a pitying smile. "Torture for you will begin in about nine years when Emma gets her period and starts having cramps and PMS. Then she'll start growing breasts and experiencing all those female problems. She'll need bras, feminine hygiene products. She'll have more interest in boys, will want to wear makeup."

Zach winced with each word spoken.

"Okay, you've done an excellent job," he groaned, putting down the pizza and burying his face in his hands. "I'm not going to survive this."

Ginna leaned forward. "I could tell you stories that would curl your hair."

"Oh, God!" His voice was muffled by his hands.

"Of course, I can't say what will happen with Trey. As a member of the male sex, you'd know much better."

"Daddy?" The objects of their conversation stood before them. Trey looked curious. "Your face is green."

Ginna smiled.

"Zach, now *that* is torture," she whispered, enunciating each word.

"Come shoot aliens with me!" Trey begged, pulling on his father's arm.

"I'm off to shoot aliens," Zach said, getting up.

"My hero. And the world will once again be safe for all mankind." Ginna chuckled.

Zach looked over his shoulder as he walked away. His expression said he wasn't sure if he was out of the woods yet.

Ginna wasn't going to forgive him all that easily.

She turned to smile at Emma, who climbed up onto her chair and picked up her slice of pizza.

"I really like my hair," she told Ginna with a big grin. "I feel grown-up now."

"It's important to feel grown-up," Ginna replied. "I'm glad I could help."

"Daddy said I can't grow up until I'm thirty. Thirty is really really old," she confided.

"Not to all of us," Ginna said dryly. "Daddies are like that. My dad said I couldn't date until I was forty."

Emma's eyes widened. "Wow. What did you do?"

She smiled. "I grew up, anyway. Emma, you're four years old and you have your whole life ahead of you. What you should do for now is enjoy your last days of preschool and go on to enjoy your time in kindergarten."

"Even Robby?" She wrinkled her nose in little-girl disgust. "He's going to the same kindergarten."

Ginna smiled. "Even Robby. You know, Emma, Robby could grow up to be a really neat guy."

"I don't think so," she said with certainty. "He picks his nose."

ZACH DIDN'T GET any more chances to talk to Ginna that night. As soon as they finished their pizza and the twins had played all the games they wanted, Ginna explained she had to get home to her dog. Which had Emma and Trey excitedly asking about Casper.

As he drove her back to the salon parking lot, she assured Emma she had the perfect hairstyle for a girl entering kindergarten and Trey would be the handsomest boy there.

For Zach, she offered a brief, faintly warm smile and a thank-you for dinner.

Emma and Trey were tired enough that they offered no argument when baths and bedtime arrived. As he tucked his daughter into bed, she reached up and gave him a tight hug.

"Thank you for letting me get a grown-up haircut, Daddy," she whispered, kissing him on the cheek.

Damn, nothing felt better.

Zach wandered around the family room, tossing toys left on the floor into the basket that sat in the corner of the room. He kept hold of one of Emma's stuffed rabbits as he dropped onto the couch, his legs splayed out in front of him.

Life was way too complicated, he decided. He was haunted by the pain in Ginna's eyes. The memory tore him up inside.

He hadn't expected what started out as a pleasant encounter on the plane to turn out to be one of the most incredible experiences of his life.

Maybe you should tell her that.

"Why don't you put a sock in it?" he growled at his conscience.

It didn't help when his gaze kept wandering in the direction of the telephone.

Would she talk to him? After the way she left him, he wouldn't be surprised if she hung up on him. Of course, he wouldn't know unless he called.

He stretched out his hand toward the phone, fingertips just barely touching the plastic back. He stretched a little more and grabbed hold of it.

He listened to the dial tone for a moment. Just to make

sure the phone worked. He made careful deliberation as he tapped out each number.

It rang twice before he heard sounds of the other end being picked up.

"Hello?"

"It's me."

Silence.

"The kids really enjoyed tonight," he began, then stopped. "That's not why I called."

More silence.

"Dammit, Ginna, I'm no good at this!" He felt frustration take over. "I thought you said you weren't mad at me anymore."

"I'm no longer mad, but I'm not going to make anything easier for you," she said quietly. "Besides, you were the one who called me."

"That's because I wanted to properly apologize to you without arcade sounds in the background," he said.

Still more silence.

"I'm waiting," she finally said. "In fact, if you're going to apologize, I suggest you do it in person. It would be more effective."

He wasn't sure if it would be more effective, as she put it. He had the good sense not to say so out loud.

"Delaney's Diner down by the wharf. Be there tomorrow morning at nine," was all she said before she hung up.

Zach hit the disconnect button.

"She can't do much bodily harm in a public place," he muttered.

ZACH REACHED the diner just a little bit before nine o'clock. The interior reflected the late fifties and sixties. Enlarged magazine advertisements from that era hung

on the wall, and classic rock and roll came from a huge
Wurlitzer jukebox. Set near the beach, the restaurant was
popular with the ocean-loving crowd.

Zach was shown to a red-benched booth and given a
brightly colored menu that featured meals named after
popular fifties' and sixties' movies and fads. He sat facing the entrance. He hadn't been here before, and he
knew he'd have to bring the twins. They'd love the music and the energy.

He watched Ginna arrive. She noticed him right away
and made her way to him, only stopping a few times to
say hello to people she knew.

Her turquoise gingham capris, yellow tank top and
matching gingham short-sleeved shirt fit the boisterous
atmosphere. Yellow backless sandals finished the outfit.

She didn't say anything as she looked at his turquoise
polo shirt, which almost perfectly matched the turquoise
in her outfit.

Her expression was blank as she sat down across from
him. She accepted a menu.

"Hey there, Ginna, coffee?" A waitress stopped by
the table.

"Hi, Rona. Yes, please." She offered a bright smile.

Rona filled her cup and looked expectantly at Zach,
who nodded.

"You know what you want?" Rona asked them.

"I'll have the Beach Party special, my eggs scrambled
and a large grapefruit juice," Ginna said.

"Palm Springs Weekend for me," Zach said after
scanning the menu. "Eggs over easy, sourdough toast,
orange juice."

Rona nodded and scooted off.

"Helpings are big here," Ginna warned him.

"Considering I barely had time for coffee this morning, big portions are a good idea," he muttered. "Trey couldn't find his backpack. Little did I know it hadn't been taken out of the truck the day before." He took a deep breath. "Here we go. Let me get this out. Then you can kill me any way you want to. I know you said you're mad at me, but I also know I hurt you. I need to make things right. As I said, Lucie told me to take the trip as this guy with no responsibilities." She arched an eyebrow. "Sometimes my sister isn't known for her spectacular ideas. But I figured why not. I didn't expect to…" He paused. "I didn't expect to meet you." He met her gaze head on. "I wasn't looking forward to that trip. I figured I'd spend my time on the beach and then nursing a bad sunburn. Instead, I got on the plane and there was a gorgeous woman sitting in my seat."

"*My* seat," she corrected.

"Obviously Luce meant it for both of us and I intend to take that up with her," he went on. "Plus, dammit, I was flattered this gorgeous woman was interested in me. I wasn't seen as Emma and Trey's dad. I was seen as this sexy guy."

"I don't recall saying you were sexy," Ginna said.

"You thought it." He wasn't going to stop now. "That was the first time in four years I've been seen that way. I liked it."

"Then might I suggest you thank your sister for her wonderful gesture."

Zach smiled. "You're right. I should. And I will. Even though she'll never let me forget it."

Ginna waved her hand in the air. "That's what sisters are for."

Rona stopped by with their glasses of juice. And soon enough, brought their food.

Ginna poured syrup over her pancakes and dug into her eggs scrambled with bits of ham and peppers.

"We've seen each other often since returning to Newport Beach," Ginna said in a low voice. "Yet you still didn't tell me about Emma and Trey."

"Which is my fault, because the last thing I would do is disavow my kids."

She held up a hand to stop him. "I believe you," she said simply. "I was hurt and I wanted you to suffer. I think you've suffered enough."

He exhaled a sigh of relief.

Ginna leaned across the table and covered his hand with hers.

"We all have secrets, Zach."

Chapter Eleven

"Did Emma still love her haircut this morning?" Ginna asked Zach.

After breakfast, he'd suggested a walk on the beach, which was only across the street.

She slipped off her sandals and dug her toes into the warm sand as she walked.

"I'm grateful for it. No tangles to comb out and her complaining I'm pulling her hair," he replied. "But yes, she still loves it. She was determined to show it off today."

Ginna stopped and looked out at the water. The breeze ruffled her hair. A few surfers were out riding the waves. When she turned back to Zach, her expression was partially hidden by her sunglasses.

"The reason I was upset had more to do with something about me than anything about you," she said candidly.

"About you?" he asked, confused.

She dropped down to sit cross-legged on the sand and patted the spot next to her. Zach sat.

"My divorce wasn't a pleasant one," she began. "In fact, nasty is probably a better word."

"Ginna, you don't—"

She held up her hand. "No, please. I have to tell you." She took a deep breath as she fought for inner strength. "One reason I divorced Denny was because he had an affair and he got his girlfriend pregnant."

Zach was stunned by her candid declaration. "And you didn't try to kill him first?"

She laughed, albeit a little ruefully. "I see you've figured out the real me."

"Obviously he didn't do well in biology if he thought he could blame you for his girlfriend's pregnancy," Zach said.

Ginna shrugged. "I was an easier target. You see, he got her pregnant when we learned I couldn't get pregnant." She stared Zach down so he would understand what she meant, then said the words she'd been dreading. "I can't have children, Zach."

"Oh, Gin." Her name came out in a soft sigh.

"No pity," she ordered. "I refused it from my family and my friends. I especially don't want it from you. It's the usual story. We tried to get pregnant. It didn't happen. We had tests. He was fine. I wasn't. He wanted kids, so he found a way to get them. He has one baby now and another on the way."

Zach's description of her ex-husband was colorful and descriptive.

"Wow, I'm impressed," she said. "I hadn't thought of some of those names."

"What about adoption?"

She shook her head. "He believed in fruit of his loins and all that."

"Sperm doesn't make a father," Zach said darkly. "He was an idiot. But I'm glad he was an idiot, because it's given me a chance with you. Even if I was an idiot, too."

"No, you weren't." Ginna felt the weight leave her shoulders.

Zach smiled. He reached for her and pulled her into his lap.

"I don't need you to do this." Her voice was muffled against his shirtfront.

"Maybe you don't need it, but I do." He rested his chin on top of her head and kept his arms tightly wrapped around her. "Just bear with me, okay?"

Ginna blinked her eyes rapidly and widened them. Anything to keep the moisture from falling. All methods failed. The warmth of his arms, his quiet acceptance of her words and his even more colorful ones about her ex meant more to her than any of the comfort she'd received in the past. She settled for resting her cheek against his chest, where she could listen to the steady beat of his heart.

"Zach?"

"Mm?"

"I'm definitely not mad at you anymore."

"SO WHEN DO WE MEET him?"

Ginna groaned. She cradled the phone between her neck and ear as she leaned forward to paint a toenail.

"Gail said he's a wonderful father," Cathy Walker told her daughter.

"Gail? How does Gail know Zach?" The moment she asked the question she was able to answer it. "Don't tell me. She's the twins' pediatrician."

"She also treats Zach's nephew. She said he's quite a handful," Cathy said. "Why not bring them over to the house next Sunday?"

"A family gathering?" Ginna was skeptical. "Is Grampa going to be there without Gramma?"

"Gramma's going with her ladies' group to see *Showboat* at the Lawrence Welk Resort," her mother said. "And you know what your grandfather thinks of musicals."

Ginna was only too aware of what her grandfather thought of musicals.

"He'll say something obnoxious to Zach." She was afraid she sounded as if she was whining.

"Zach, I'm sure, can go toe-to-toe with Grampa. Better than Denny did."

"And Grampa will enjoy saying he was right about Denny."

"He was."

"I warned him the last time that if he brings it up again, no more free haircuts." Ginna leaned forward again, painting another nail a delicate lavender shade. She arched back to study the effect. Perfect.

"We'll see all of you about ten," Cathy told her. "The kids will love having someone new to play with."

Ginna hung up, defeated as always. She tapped out Zach's phone number. She might as well get it over with.

The moment she heard his hello, she rushed on, "I hope you don't have any plans for Sunday afternoon, because you've been invited to the Walker family gathering. I can promise you it will be scary as hell, but Emma and Trey will love it. Anyone under the age of ten loves it out there. Lucie and Nick are also invited. But don't feel you have to go," she added.

"What time do I pick you up?"

"TALK ABOUT COINCIDENCES," Lucie said as Zach drove down the freeway that Sunday. "Gail being Ginna's sister-in-law and all."

"Yes, isn't it? Not to mention you being one of

Ginna's clients. You setting up Ginna's and my trips. Ginna and I ending up with the same seat assignment. Wild, huh?''

"That was something," Lucie replied, unperturbed. "And they claim computers can't make mistakes. How extended is this family of yours, Ginna?'' she asked as if realizing it was a good time to redirect the conversation.

"My brothers' families and friends and their families show up. Sometimes my parents' friends stop by. There's touch football, baseball, water polo or volleyball games," Ginna replied. "There's usually a couple of teenagers willing to look after the younger kids by the pool or organize some games for them. My brothers work different shifts at the fire department, which means there're people from both of those. And some paramedics. We're always well covered for medical help between them and Gail. Dad will show off his beloved cars. Mom will decide you need feeding. The usual.''

"And you have a swimming pool!'' Trey shouted in earsplitting tones, jumping up and down as far as his car seat would allow.

Ginna looked at Zach. "It's a shame Emma and Trey aren't excited about going," she remarked dryly. "And yet Nick is downright ecstatic.''

The object of their conversation sat in the rear with his mother, looking as if this was his last day on earth. He held his comic book up to his face.

"I didn't think geniuses read comic books," she whispered.

"They do if they're trying to figure out what all the attraction is," he whispered back. "So far, he's read about a thousand of them. He's decided to come up with the ultimate hero that will outsell every comic book printed.''

"Everyone needs a goal," she said philosophically.

As Zach followed Ginna's directions, he enjoyed the view of large homes on equally large pieces of property.

He parked behind a minivan in an area that resembled a small parking lot. Then they all started getting out of the Pathfinder.

"Do you have horses?" Emma asked, hopping up and down in an attempt to see everywhere.

"Sorry, sweetie, no horses, but my dad keeps some really cool battery-operated miniature cars for you munchkins to drive," Ginna told her.

"Do you have dogs?" Trey was doing his own share of looking.

"Dogs we have," she promised.

"Great, Em will want to take home a car and Trey will try to smuggle a dog in the truck," Zach groaned, already fearing the worst.

"Hello, darling." A lovely older woman whom Ginna would look like in twenty-five or thirty years walked up and hugged her. She turned to the others and smiled. "I'm Cathy, Ginna's mother. You must be Zach, Emma, Trey, Lucie and Nick." She smiled at each of them. "I'm glad you could come."

"As if you'd miss us in this crowd," Ginna teased, slipping an arm around her mother's waist.

"I always know who's here and who isn't," Cathy said serenely. "Come along and meet the rest of the family."

Zach had no idea what he was in for as he was escorted from one group to another, meeting Ginna's brothers again, along with some of their friends and co-workers, and her younger sister, Nikki. He'd barely warned the twins to behave before Cathy smoothly inserted them in a group of young children overseen by a teenage girl.

"Everything will be fine," she told him. "Marcie is wonderful at keeping track of the children. Their parents don't have to worry about them."

"Obviously you haven't met Nick," Lucie said.

"He'll be fine, too." Cathy patted her shoulder. "Come have some lemonade."

Ginna perked up. "Mom, you made some of your infamous lemonade?"

"It seemed like a good day for it."

"This lemonade has a kick to it," she warned Lucie.

"Sounds good to me." Lucie perked up.

Ginna stopped by a large washtub filled with ice, beer cans and bottles. She snagged three bottles and handed two to Lucie and Zach.

"Mom makes it easy for us by putting her butt-kicking lemonade in bottles," she explained.

He barely opened the bottle before Brian and Mark advanced on him. The two brothers were grinning broadly.

"Good to see you!" Brian boomed, clapping him on the back. "I gotta say, the best thing you can do out here is escape the women."

"I heard that!" Gail Roberts Walker shouted. She held a baby cradled against her shoulder. Her dark-blond hair was cut in a smooth curve that was tucked behind her ears. Her only jewelry was a diamond wedding set on her ring finger and a chain with two gemstones gracing the chain. Zach already knew the stones were Brian and baby Jenny's birthstones.

Brian immediately loped over to his wife and took the

baby out of her arms, gently settling the tiny bundle against his large chest.

"It's just an act for the guys, honey," he said.

Judging by the smile on her lips, she didn't believe it for a minute.

Brian returned with his small bundle. "Come on, I'll introduce you to the guys," he told Zach.

"Hey there, gorgeous," Mark greeted Lucie. "You wanna fool around?"

She smiled, not taking offense. "You wanna broken foot?"

He shuddered theatrically. "I can see you won't be easy."

"That's what all my dates say," she said sweetly. "Tell me something? Do you like blinding people with your choice of clothing?" She gestured to his bright red-and-yellow Hawaiian-print shirt, so unlike his two brothers' sedate navy T-shirts with the fire department insignia.

"Whatever catches your attention." He grinned.

"Go away, Mark," Ginna said. "She's much too smart to have anything to do with you."

Mark looked at Lucie. "You don't want me to go away, do you?"

She smiled at him. "Trust me. I'm too much woman for you."

Ginna snickered.

Mark inclined his head in silent tribute. "I'll catch you later," he told Lucie.

Lucie chuckled. "Not if I can help it."

As Zach was led away by the three Walker brothers, he heard Cathy ask Ginna a question, and he was positive his name was mentioned. Unfortunately he couldn't hear her reply.

"So who's the cute blonde who came with you? Ginna wouldn't introduce us." Mark asked Zach. "Those shorts sure do a lot for her—"

"She's my sister," Zach said, injecting pure threat into his tone.

Mark nodded. One thing he understood was protecting a sister's virtue.

"Nice going, bonehead." Brian slapped the back of Mark's head with his free hand. The baby didn't open her eyes, as if she was used to her daddy punishing her uncle. "You knew Zach was bringing his sister and nephew with him."

"So sue me. I forgot." Mark shrugged.

"How old is your daughter?" Zach asked Brian, recalling the times he carried a tiny Emma and Trey that same way.

"Almost seven months. Top of her class," said the proud father. "She even sleeps through the night."

"Best thing that can happen. Emma and Trey may have slept through the night, but I still didn't. I don't think I slept more than an hour at a time until they were a year old. I was always afraid something would happen to them. Gail told me I was overreacting, but I couldn't make myself believe it," Zach said.

Brian introduced Zach to the group of men. Fellow firemen Kurt and Rick saluted him with their beer bottles. When Zach answered Kurt's question about his occupation, Mark slapped his forehead.

"That's where I saw your name!" he exclaimed. "You write some downright scary stuff about being a single father. You're a stronger man than I am."

"Think how it was for me," Zach joked.

"Okay, daddies," Jeff cut in. "We're trying to have man talk here."

"Twin girls and a baby boy," Brian explained. "Jeff's idea of man talk is complaining Abby doesn't have any time for him."

"Can it, Walker!" A stunning blond woman shouted from a nearby group. White shorts showed off long tanned legs, and a lacy pink tank top showed off the rest of a showstopping figure.

"Jeff's ball and chain," Mark confided in a whisper. "She's not too bright, though. If she'd been smarter, she would have chosen me. Hey!" He rubbed the back of his head. As Abby Walker passed by him, she'd taken the time to smack the back of his head. "I'm getting a concussion here."

"Maybe some smarts will find their way in, then," she drawled. "Hi, Zach. I'm sure you're more intelligent than any of these animals here. Your son is charming my girls."

"My girls, too," Jeff inserted with mock hurt.

She ignored her husband as she concentrated on Zach. "Luckily for all of us they take after me." She reached up and pinched his mouth between her fingertips. "If you do anything to hurt my sister-in-law, I will tear your mouth off and feed it to you," she said in a soft voice. "Understood?"

He bobbed his head, since he was unable to say a word.

"Damn," Brian breathed. "She'd do it, too."

"That's my Abby. Such a delicate sensitive creature," Jeff said.

Abby turned to Brian and took the baby out of his arms. "The last thing this darling girl needs to hear is any of your guy stuff. Besides, it's time for her nap." She walked off, carrying the baby.

Zach blinked. "Did we just have an earthquake?" He looked at the other men for confirmation.

"Seems like it, doesn't it?" Mark grinned. "Abby's a force unto herself. But you gotta love her. Like a sister," he said hastily, catching his brother's glare. "I think of her the way I think of Ginna. And the Black Plague."

"One day, Mark, you will meet a woman who will totally bowl you over," Brian said. "And I want to be there for the show."

"No way." He shook his head. "Someone's got to be smart here. I'm going to spend my old age as the eccentric bachelor uncle."

Zach soon relaxed and was drawn into a baseball game. Kurt and Rick welcomed him with shouts they were going to win.

"So how are you with a bat and ball?" Ginna asked, taking his beer can from him.

"I won't embarrass you."

She batted her eyelashes. "Hit a home run and I will give you…" she whispered in his ear.

The temperature suddenly shot up a good hundred degrees.

"That old fantasy," she went on softly. "You, the big jock. Me, the perky cheerleader."

"Talk about incentive," he said, moving over to the team he was playing on.

Zach quickly learned that the Walker men and their friends played a no-holds-barred game of ball. Catcalls were fast and furious from the sidelines, and the women acting as cheerleaders added another element to the game.

Ginna, in pink paisley-print cotton shorts and a pink

tank top, was colorful as she leaped and cheered every time Zach was up at bat.

He found he had to concentrate on watching the ball and not Ginna, who was teaching Emma how to make high kicks.

In the end, his team won by two runs. Ginna whooped and ran over, leaping onto him and wrapping her legs around his waist. She kissed him. He grabbed hold of her to keep his balance and kissed her back.

He was vaguely aware of joking shouts directed their way.

"My hero," she murmured as he set her back down.

"Hey, that's my sister you're fondling," Mark protested.

"He was dropped on the head as a child," Ginna told Zach. "We just ignore him when he gets like that."

"Maybe if you'd dropped him again, he might have ended up normal," Lucie said. "As for my darling brother—" she looped an arm around his neck and kissed him on the cheek "—he led his baseball team to the championships in college," she said proudly, still hugging him.

"I caught a ball," Mark told her, greatly offended at being left out.

"And promptly dropped it," Ginna said.

"Zach, if you're this good at baseball, then I want you on my team for water polo," Jeff told him, clapping him on the back. "Mark really sucks at it, like he does at baseball." He laughed, ducking as his brother playfully swung a fist at him.

"Come on, Dad's fired up the barbecue. Red meat for you," Ginna told Zach, pulling him away.

"Grampa's with him," Jeff yelled after them. "He's supervising the fire."

Zach didn't miss Ginna's grimace. "Something I should know?" he asked, tucking his hand in the back pocket of her shorts.

"Grampa is my dad's father, and while I love him dearly, he can be a bit much at times," she explained. "Emma and Trey will love him because he carries candies, and he's about the best grandfather a kid can ask for. We all love him to pieces and there're times we want to cut him into pieces."

"So where'd you learn those shimmy moves you were doing on the sidelines?" he asked as they returned to the patio and over toward a large barbecue pit. He could see two older men standing by the grill. Their stance was that of two roosters battling over who ruled the farmyard.

Both men were dressed in T-shirts. One had hair more silver than brown and the same blue eyes that declared him a Walker. The other man, with his white hair and deeply tanned face creased by time and weather, showed just where the Walker good looks came from. Father and son greeted Ginna with broad smiles.

"Like my moves, did ya, Zach?" She bumped him with her hip. "There're my two favorite men!" She ran over and hugged each of them.

"When're you bringing the baby in for a tune-up?" the older one asked.

"Next week, Grampa. Dad, Grampa, this is Zach Stone. Zach, my dad, Lou, my grandfather, Theo."

Lou's smile was warm and open, while Theo looked at Zach with blazing blue eyes that seemed to see right through.

"Your son has good taste," he said to Zach. "He told me my Model T was a beauty."

"He has an extensive Matchbox collection. They're his favorite toys," Zach replied.

Theo sniffed with disdain. "Toys. He needs to be around the real thing."

"Grampa feels if you don't get grease and oil under your fingernails by the time you're three, you're lost to the trade forever. So why aren't you with Gramma like all the other husbands are with their wives?"

"Ha!" he snorted. "Most of the men were smart like me and stayed home." He peered at the grill. "Aren't those ready to flip over?"

Lou sighed and turned the burgers. The ones already cooked were stacked on a plate and handed to one of the teenage girls in charge of the younger children. She smiled her thanks and headed for the tables that had been set up.

"You run quite an operation here," Zach said.

"The kids believed in bringing their friends by and we never minded it. We knew where our kids were, and with their friends welcome, there was never a lack of anything to do," Lou replied. "It's not as if we don't have the room. We've got about fifteen acres, more than we need. We're all family here."

Zach looked over to where Emma and Trey were happily consuming hamburgers. A few of the children around them appeared to be their age. He'd always been relieved that they never had a problem in groups. Looking at them, he could see they would thrive in this atmosphere.

When he turned to Ginna, he noticed something else. She, too, was looking at the children's tables. The smile on her lips held a hint of sorrow that was reflected in her eyes.

I can never have children, he recalled her sorrowful

words spoken with bravery. Ginna might have said that she'd leave it to her brothers and sister to expand the Walker family, but deep down, she mourned the fact that she herself couldn't contribute.

As he turned from her, he met Lou's eyes. The older man's expression told him he knew exactly what Zach was feeling. Lou gave a barely perceptible nod, including him in the sadness the family shared.

Being with Ginna made him a part of this family. Even Lucie was included just that easily. Their own parents had never made their children's friends this welcome.

"You're a very generous man, Lou," he said quietly.

The older man grinned. "My wife'll tell you I'm pretty much crazy. But if pressed, she'd tell you she loves it, too. There's nothing more she likes than feeding a bunch of people."

"Everyone brings food," Ginna explained. "Mom makes cakes that are fantastic. Penny over there makes great coleslaw. I get off easy because I usually give a few haircuts while I'm here." She picked up two plates and held them out. Theo dropped buns on the plates while Lou set the burgers on them. "Thanks." She kissed both men's cheeks and led Zach off. She kept up a running commentary on choice of foods as they moved down the tables laden with salads and various condiments for their hamburgers. By the time they headed for a place to sit and eat, his plate was overloaded.

"I'll never eat all this," he said as they sat at a table.

"Yes, you will," she said confidently, lifting her hamburger to her mouth. "You need the energy. There's even more going on after lunch."

"If you do any more of those shimmy movements, there'll be a hell of a lot going on, but nothing you want your parents to see," he murmured.

She arched an eyebrow. "Oh, you'd be amazed what my parents have seen," she said in a low voice. "Especially with my brothers."

"Telling stories again?" Brian asked, taking a seat across from them. Gail smiled a hello and slipped in beside him. "Gin's got one of those overactive imaginations," he confided.

Lucie took one of the open spaces, then glared at Mark who sat down next to her.

"Keep it up, brother dearest," Ginna said sweetly. "I still have some of those damning pictures locked away. I'm sure Gail would enjoy seeing them."

"Really?" Gail grinned at her sister-in-law. "How good?"

Ginna leaned forward, acting as if no one else was around. "Let's just say that some of these photographs do not show him at his best," she said in a mock whisper. She looked around as if making sure no one was eavesdropping. "We'll talk later."

Gail nodded, then turned to Zach. "The twins look great. Obviously they've recovered from the chicken pox."

"After those first few days, they sailed through it. I was the wreck," he confessed.

"I've treated Emma and Trey since they were born," Gail explained to the others. "So far, they've fared better than Zach has."

"I always thought Jeff acted sappy about his girls until our daughter was born," Brian said. "I'm already having nightmares about when Jenny starts dating."

"I'm not letting Emma date until she's thirty," Zach said.

Brian nodded. "Sounds good to me."

Later on, Ginna took Zach on a tour of the house.

Walking through the large home, he realized the interior was as well set up for entertaining as the exterior was.

"And now for the pièce de résistance," she announced with a theatrical flourish, opening a door near the end of the hall.

Zach didn't need an explanation to know the bedroom he was looking at belonged to a younger Ginna. The turquoise-and-lime accents had him thinking of the Caribbean. The white wood furniture was that of a young girl, while pictures, pennants and movie posters were for Ginna the teenager. He turned around and found her leaning against the now-closed door.

"I bet your dad would get out his shotgun if he knew I was in your room," he said, grinning at her.

She shrugged. "Daddy's a lousy shot. He's always the first victim in a paint-ball battle." She smiled slowly. "Does this bring back old memories, Zach? Did you ever sneak into a girlfriend's bedroom while you were in high school?" She walked toward him with a slight shimmy to her hips, which he found mesmerizing.

"Obviously you never met the girl I dated in high school," he replied. "I wasn't allowed to kiss her until we'd dated for four months."

"Wow." She widened her eyes. "And you kept on seeing her?"

"I guess I figured she was worth waiting for when it came to a kiss." He watched Ginna move even closer.

"Was she?" She stopped when her breasts brushed against his chest. She tipped her head back, her lips parted.

He wrapped his hand around the back of her neck. "Sweetheart, she was nothing compared to you." He moved his mouth over hers in a slow easy motion.

She lifted her arms, looping them around his neck as she kissed him back.

"You could fulfill one of my fantasies," she murmured.

"And that is?"

"Making out with my boyfriend in my bedroom while my parents are outside."

Zach's smile said it all. He dipped his head and placed a trail of butterfly kisses along her collarbone.

"Funny. That was my fantasy, too."

Chapter Twelve

"You're a good guy, Zach," Brian told him as they gathered all the children later that day. His blue eyes turned the color of steel. "But if you hurt my sister, I will make sure no one ever finds one piece of your body."

Zach looked over to where Ginna stood talking to several women. She held Emma perched on one hip with the little girl's head drooping wearily against her shoulder, and Trey held on to Ginna's other hand, but his body leaned against her.

He turned back to Brian. "If I did something as stupid as hurt her, I'd deserve anything you'd want to do to me. Although—" he matched Brian's intense expression "—if you were going to tear someone to pieces, you should have done it to her ex."

The other man studied him closely. "So she told you." His face broke out into a grin. "It took a while, but Denny learned to keep his mouth shut."

One of those man-to-man looks passed between them. Zach's lips stretched in a smile. "Damn, I wish I'd been there."

"Mark thought we should videotape it, but Jeff and I

talked him out of it. It was a good conversation and we got our point across.''

Gail walked by, and as she did, she touched her husband's shoulder. Zach saw the love flow between them and envied their connection. He caught a movement out of the corner of his eye and realized Ginna was walking his way. He reached to take Emma out of her arms, but she shook her head. He leaned down and swung Trey into his arms. The little boy closed his eyes and draped himself over his dad's shoulder.

''I don't wanna go,'' Trey muttered sleepily.

''By the time I get you in the truck, you'll be sound asleep,'' he told his son, rubbing his back. The little boy's body quickly grew slack with weariness bordering on sleep.

''Can I drive?'' Nick asked, walking up with his mother.

''Not in my lifetime,'' Zach said.

The boy looked up. ''You are so reaching middle age.''

Zach looked at Lucie. ''Make him stop.''

''Both of you behave.'' She herded her son toward Zach's SUV.

After the kids were belted in, Lucie looked at Zach. ''If you want, I can take the twins tonight,'' she offered.

Ginna shook her head. ''I'm giving a perm to a co-worker in the morning.''

The drive to Ginna's house was quiet as the kids slept.

''Your family knows how to throw a great barbecue,'' Lucie said. ''Thank you for inviting us.''

''We don't believe in doing anything small,'' Ginna replied. ''Even if my family can be a bit much at times.''

When Zach walked Ginna to her front door, they

heard Casper's excited barks from inside. She shushed the dog as she turned to Zach.

"I'm glad you came," she said with a tiny smile. "I just hope my brothers didn't beat up on you too much."

"No more than I might have deserved for making love to their sister," he said. He dipped his head and gave her a kiss that lingered on her lips. "Are you free for dinner night after next? The kids are going to a friend's house for a birthday party sleepover."

Her lips tilted upward. "Hmm, the children at a sleep-over and you free for dinner. How convenient. Now, we *are* talking dinner ending with a rich calorie-laden dessert, aren't we?"

"Whatever chocolate confection you want."

"Two?" she pressed.

"Three. You can even eat mine." He grinned.

"Then I'm free, but you might want to bring Casper a bone. He's been giving you those looks lately," she whispered.

"Got it." He kissed her again. "Seven? Here or the salon?"

Ginna thought for a moment. "I'll have to call you and let you know." She unlocked the door. "Good night, Zach."

"Good night." He waited until she slipped inside and he heard the click of the dead bolt. Casper's excited barks told him she was being lovingly assaulted by her dog.

By the time he reached his truck, Lucie had moved into the passenger seat.

"She's got a nice family," she murmured as he pulled away from the curb.

"Yeah, they're something else," he said. "Did I see Mark putting the moves on you?"

Lucie shrugged. "He asked me to go to a basketball game with him."

"And?"

"I told him I'd rather eat dirt. I also told him he's obnoxious, arrogant and has an ego the size of Australia," she replied.

Zach laughed. "And he said?"

"He just looked at me until I explained the meaning of the words *obnoxious, arrogant* and *ego.*" She rolled her eyes. "He thought ego was a body part. I think you can figure that one out."

"No wonder Ginna said he was dropped on his head when he was a baby."

Zach couldn't contain his grin. He couldn't remember the last time his sister had been interested in a man, and even though she'd cut out her tongue before she'd admit it, she was definitely interested in Mark Walker.

He made a mental note to warn the guy off her. Or he would have to hurt him.

GINNA COULDN'T SLEEP. After the day she'd had, she should have crawled into bed and been out the second her head hit the pillow. Instead, she lay curled up on her side, staring at the open window, the sheer curtains blowing softly in the breeze. Casper lay on his self-appointed spot at the end of the bed. Every once in a while he whined and twitched, so she imagined he was dreaming about the cute poodle next door.

Reliving the day was easy.

Watching Zach play baseball, enjoying his grins and enthusiasm for the game as he played hard to make sure his team won.

Watching Emma and Trey run and play with the other kids as easily as if they'd known them all their lives.

Even Nick did his best to convince a few of the boys that building a rocket was easy. And almost succeeded.

But it was the time she and Zach spent in her old bedroom that took up a good deal of space in her heart.

Her smile refused to go away as she relived that time.

All those adolescent dreams she'd had in that room. Stories she'd spun in her head of a handsome prince stealing into her room to make mad passionate love to her.

Little did she know the day would arrive when that dream would come true.

She had an idea a few members of her family suspected something had happened—she and Zach were gone so long—but no one said anything. Even Mark had kept quiet. She suspected Abby had something to do with that, bless her.

She'd been leery of going there today. Since her divorce it hadn't been easy to attend gatherings like that. Family, friends. And all the children. Reminders of what she couldn't have.

She could put on a brave front, say that Denny's words hadn't hurt her. That she could go on even if she couldn't have children. If they knew she was lying through her teeth, no one ever challenged her. She loved them even more for all the warm unconditional support they offered.

Denny's words had hurt. He'd told her she was flawed. He'd made her feel almost deformed.

I'm sorry, Ginna, but the tests have shown you and Denny cannot have children, the doctor had told her. He'd gone on to say maybe, but a big maybe, in vitro fertilization could be an option. But she'd shut down by then. What was the use when he said there was little chance the procedure would work.

The test results were in an envelope in her desk. She hadn't bothered reading them fully. She knew enough of what they said.

As Denny told her, she couldn't give him his own children. So what if she was beautiful and even pretty smart? She couldn't do the one important thing he'd counted on. So he went out and found someone who could.

She rolled onto her other side and punched her pillow into submission. Casper raised his head, then lowered it and fell back to sleep.

She envied his ease in sleeping and wished slumber would come as easily for her. She wasn't her best early in the morning, and going in early to give Cheryl a perm was going to be difficult enough for her.

Today showed her more of what Zach was like as a father. She saw Zach's pride in his children and their ease with making new friends.

He was excellent father material and he deserved more children. He had more than enough love to share.

But that wasn't something she could give him. It wasn't fair to even think about a future with him when she couldn't give him what he warranted.

After her divorce, she'd had a good long talk with herself, and at the time decided she was better off remaining alone. Maybe a long-term relationship if the right man came along, but she was going to be careful that her heart didn't get involved.

Then she'd met Zach, who took her to a fairy-tale brunch. Who admitted he wouldn't hurt her for anything. Who knew she couldn't have children and didn't consider her less than a real woman the way Denny had. He'd listened to her, sat there on the beach and comforted her without offering pity. He held her in his arms and told her she was never to think there was anything wrong with her. He made her feel whole again.

"You were the loser, Denny," Ginna said out loud. "Just because I have a defective uterus doesn't mean I'm a defective person."

She thought saying it aloud would make it true in her mind.

It didn't.

"INSTEAD OF GOING OUT, come over and I'll cook for you," Ginna offered when she called Zach that Tuesday afternoon.

"Are you sure your dog will allow me to eat in the house?" he joked.

"If you bring him a bone, he'll be your friend for life."

"Yes, but I expect to live another fifty years or so. He might have other ideas. What time do you want me over there?"

She glanced at her calendar and estimated what time she would get home and be able to start cooking. "Six-thirty. Afterward, we can play strip Scrabble," she said in a low voice.

"I think I'll dig out my dictionary and get some studying in," he said huskily.

"You do that."

The minute Ginna hung up, she jotted down a few ideas for dinner. She sank onto the couch in the staff-only area and stretched out.

"You're cooking for the man?" Nora shook her head in amazement. "This must be it." She looked toward the ceiling. "Why can't I take a trip and find a guy like that?"

"The last guy you met was arrested in the midst of

your date,'' Cheryl reminded her as she sat at the table, nibbling on her salad. ''Was it two or three felonies he was wanted for?''

''Who counted? It was bad enough he'd stolen the car he'd picked me up in,'' Nora groaned. ''I swear I'm a magnet for losers. If I had any brains at all, I'd just give up on all men.''

''What about that guy you met at the farmers' market last weekend?'' Cheryl asked.

''He's an artist who felt he was destined to be more famous than Picasso, Rembrandt and Van Gogh all wrapped up in one. He's looking for an investor. Namely, a woman who will pay all his bills,'' Nora told them. ''Any idea of a romance was gone when I told him I was color blind.''

Ginna frowned. ''I thought it was only men who could be color blind.''

Nora smirked. ''Amazing that an artist didn't realize that, isn't it?''

''Blind Date Central is having another wedding,'' Cheryl announced. ''One of my clients found her true love on the bulletin board. She said she took one look at his picture and knew he was the one. I guess he felt the same way. They're getting married next month.'' She shot Nora a look filled with sympathy. ''The groom is one of the men you had found there.''

Everyone held their breath. Ginna stood behind Nora holding up one finger, then two. The third barely lifted before the hairdresser exploded.

She stomped around the room like a blond hurricane. She cast curses on every man she'd known since grade school, damned the male sex in general and then went on to call herself a few choice names. It stopped as suddenly as it began. She dropped, exhausted, onto a chair.

''Which son of a bitch?'' she asked quietly.

Cheryl winced. ''She said his name was Bill.''

Nora spun around and stared at her. ''Bill? You're kidding. He works for an investment firm?''

''I think she said he did.''

Nora threw her head back and laughed. ''Maybe she doesn't know yet.''

''Know what?'' Ginna asked.

Nora gasped as she continued laughing. ''We'd only dated a couple times and I never took his card off the board. I realized afterward I should have. I went to take it off, but it was already gone. Maybe it won't bother her as much.''

Ginna playfully pounded on her co-worker's head. ''What won't bother her?'' she demanded.

''The reason I stopped dating him was I found him in my bedroom trying on my underwear. When I threw him out, he asked if he could keep a couple pair. I burned them, instead.'' She wrinkled her nose in distaste.

Cheryl started laughing. ''We're definitely talking a match made in heaven. She's a lingerie buyer for Saks.''

Ginna shook her head. ''And on that note, I'm going out before my client arrives.'' She dropped her empty water bottle in the recycling container. As she left the room, she could hear her friends discuss the male sex in more unflattering terms than flattering.

''Oh, Zach, you have no idea how lucky you are that Lucie didn't put you up on that board,'' she murmured.

''A GIFT GUARANTEED to make any dog happy,'' the butcher assured Zach, wrapping up a bone that Zach could swear came from a dinosaur.

Zach followed instructions and cooked the bone first. Emma and Trey gave him mournful gazes when they heard he was going to Ginna's for dinner. Especially since the bone he bought was for Ginna's dog.

"You have been looking forward to this sleepover at Erin and Michael's for the past two weeks," he reminded them, naming friends who were also fraternal twins and celebrating their birthday with a sleepover. Zach shuddered at the thought of overseeing ten kids at a sleepover.

"But we like Ginna, too." Emma pouted. She crossed her arms in front of her chest in a pose Zach was only too familiar with.

"And you will see her, but you already told your friends you'd be at the birthday sleepover and you are going," he said firmly. "They're expecting the two of you to attend. Before now, it was all you two could talk about."

Emma released a soulful sigh. "Okay, we'll go, but we'd still rather go with you and Ginna." With her brother in tow, she marched off to her room to get ready for the party.

Zach turned away so his children couldn't see his grin.

"A performance worthy of an Academy Award," he murmured.

He dropped them off at the party and drove on to Ginna's house. She greeted him with a smile and a kiss on the lips.

"Oh, my." She eyed the two packages he carried.

"One is yours," he told her.

"Gee, what I've always wanted," she quipped, holding up the meaty beef bone.

"That's for Casper. The other one is yours."

She handed him back the bone and called the dog. Casper came running and skidded to a stop. He eyed Zach with canine suspicion.

"Hey, boy, look what I have for you." He held out the bone.

The German shepherd lifted his head, sniffing the air. He stepped forward and delicately took the bone from Zach. As he stepped back, he didn't take his eyes off the man. His expression told Zach he was taking the bone, but he was still reserving his judgment about him.

"I told you all it took was giving him a bone." Ginna beamed at two of her favorite males.

"Better that one than my leg," he muttered.

Ginna gestured for him to follow her. As she headed for the kitchen, she peeked inside the pink cardboard box. Her squeal echoed off the walls.

"I gather you like what you see." He grinned.

"When I said bring chocolate, I had no idea you'd go for something this sinful," she cooed, setting the box on the counter. "Would you like something to drink? Wine, beer, soft drink?"

"Wine sounds good." He sat at the table. "The kids weren't too happy at not being invited tonight. All of a sudden a sleepover at what they consider the coolest house in town wasn't all that exciting."

"Why is it the coolest house in town?" she asked, pulling a bottle of wine out of the refrigerator and two glasses out of the cabinet.

"These friends are another set of fraternal twins. Their dad produces a couple of popular sitcoms and their mom is an actress." He named names that had her widening her eyes with awe. "Despite their hectic schedules, they always get involved in the kids' activities. At Halloween they had a costume party complete with a haunted house that scared four-year-olds without terrorizing them. They also have enough pets to qualify as a small zoo. Pretty much like your family's house."

"Ah." She nodded her head in understanding as she

poured the wine. "It does sound familiar. Except the bottled water they serve is probably European."

"Flown in especially for the occasion," he said glibly, accepting the glass.

She picked up the other glass and sat across from him. "Sounds as if they'll have a ball."

"They will."

"But I'm flattered they wanted to come over." Ginna smiled. She sipped her wine. "They're wonderful."

"They were well behaved on Sunday," he corrected. "Cathy said she'd take them any day."

"Believe me, she doesn't say that lightly," Ginna told him. "She and Dad love to spoil kids."

Zach looked down as she crossed her legs. The colorful pink-purple-and-navy sarong-style skirt parted, revealing her bare legs. Her purple knit tank top completed the outfit.

"I made sweet-and-sour-chicken," she told him. "It should be ready soon."

"Just as long as I don't have to use chopsticks. I really suck at chopsticks," he confessed. "I usually end up with more food in my lap than in my mouth."

She clucked her tongue. "Then you're just not using them right." She got up and rummaged through cabinets and drawers. She returned with plates and silverware, along with one set of chopsticks. She turned back around when the timer dinged.

"Anything I can do to help?" he asked.

Ginna shook her head. With quick efficient movements, she had the chicken, vegetables and rice in serving dishes and set on the table.

"I am so glad I didn't have time to eat lunch." He hungrily eyed the large array of food she'd laid out on the table. He watched her deftly handle her chopsticks, easily picking up morsels of food.

When Zach started in on his second helping, Ginna grabbed her chopsticks and moved around the table. She sat sideways on his lap, so she could face him and still reach the table.

"The last time we did this you were feeding me breakfast," Zach murmured, circling her waist with his hands.

"My, my, you do bring out my domestic side," she teased, half turning. She picked up a piece of chicken and held it to his lips. "See how easy it is?" she said softly, choosing a piece of vegetable.

"Sure, it's easy when you're doing it." He opened his mouth for a snow pea next.

When she started to turn away, he stopped her and brought her mouth to his, instead.

"Even better," he disclosed, sliding his tongue along her bottom lip.

"You still have more food," she said.

"I think I'd rather have you." He cradled her in his arms as he stood up. His memory served him well as he made his way to her bedroom.

He placed her on the bed. She raised herself on her knees to reach for his shirt. In no time she'd pulled it over his head and tossed it across the room. Her tank top quickly followed, along with his pants.

"Did I ever tell you that you are the sexiest woman I have ever met?" Zach asked, bending over her, his hands braced on either side of her.

Her eyes danced with laughter meant to warm him inside and out. "Not lately, so perhaps you should remind me." Her laughter wrapped around him just as her arms wrapped around his shoulders.

"My pleasure." He followed her down onto the bed.

"Oh, Zach," she breathed in his ear. "If you do it right, it will be *our* pleasure."

Zach found the tie that released Ginna's skirt. His heart slammed against his rib cage when he saw the purple bikini panties.

"Damn. I think I just swallowed my tongue."

"Not allowed." She framed his face with her hands and pulled it down to her. "That's my job," she whispered, layering his skin with butterfly kisses. "You turn me into a wild woman, Zachary Stone. With you, I want to be the ultimate sex fantasy."

"I wouldn't worry. I think you've more than accomplished it." He found the spot just behind her ear that he knew caused her to shiver with pleasure. Her skin was cool to the touch but quickly turned to warm silk.

Zach had never thought much of foreplay. He knew it was probably a guy thing. Women liked to cuddle. Most men didn't.

With Ginna, he wanted to savor every inch of her as long as possible. He never wanted his time with her to end.

"So sweet," he mumbled, pursing his mouth around a dark-rose nipple. She moaned his name as he suckled. "Mine." He grasped her hips and brought her up against him. "Gorgeous." He rubbed his hips against hers.

"You are a maniac!" She laughed.

"Hey, laughter is not a good idea when a man is on a totally serious mission." He swooped up and covered her mouth with his. His tongue invaded her mouth, enticing her to play. She gracefully accepted his invitation.

"Consider it joyful laughter," she said, tilting back her head. Her hands never stopped fluttering down his spine, tracing the ridges and indentations.

He looked down at her face. Her skin was flushed with desire, her eyes luminous with the joy she just confessed to. The expression on her face backed up her avowal and lifted him the way no drug or any amount of alcohol ever could.

"Good," he said huskily, "because, lady, you make me so damn happy I don't know how I contain it."

Her smile grew wider. "Then don't contain. Let it out. Share with me."

Zach leaned down and reached for his pants. When he brought up a foil packet and started to open it, she stayed his motion.

There was the faintest tremor in her smile, an almost unnatural brightness to her eyes.

"I want to feel you," she murmured. "It's not as if we need to worry about anything."

His gut tightened with a brief spasm. There was nothing he wanted to do more than give her what *she* wanted. Something he wasn't able to give.

But he could give her himself. And he would.

He moved back over her, then rolled until she straddled him. He grasped her hips and guided her on top of him. She bent forward to kiss him deeply as her inner muscles tightened around him.

She moved slowly, teasing him with kisses and soft licks, her inner muscles drawing him in even deeper.

Zach gritted his teeth against the pleasurable pain Ginna inflicted on him. He felt the electric sensation zing from the middle of his body straight to his brain. He wasn't sure he could take much more and said so.

"Oh, my darling, I think it's only begun," she whispered, biting down gently on his lower lip.

Zach seemed to shift into automatic drive. The need for completion was there, but Ginna alternately teased and tantalized him. He'd put her in charge and she took the role seriously.

Until they both could no longer hold back. Her breathing quickened at the same time his did.

Zach felt the world revolve, then shoot them out into myriad bright colors.

And then he knew nothing but the woman who loved him so thoroughly.

"ARE YOU SURE you're not a succubus?" Zach asked Ginna once he regained his senses. She lay curled up in his arms, her cheek resting against his chest.

"You're still alive, aren't you?" She straightened up. "Are you hungry?"

His eyes gleamed with pure devilment. "I'd say you pretty much took care of that appetite."

She rolled her eyes. She hopped off the bed and snatched up his polo shirt, pulling it over her head.

Zach lay back, since there wasn't much he could do. To say the woman wore him out was not understating his condition.

He could hear faint sounds coming from the kitchen, could hear the French doors open and close as she let her dog outside.

In a few moments she returned carrying a glass of wine and a large plate with a good-size portion of the dessert he'd brought. She plopped down on the bed, sitting cross-legged beside him.

She forked off a piece of the multilayer chocolate cake and brought it to her lips. She closed her eyes and uttered a moan that Zach swore he'd heard only a few moments before. He started grinning.

"This is so good!" Ginna forked off another piece and fed him. "You are so lucky I'm sharing this with you. What do they call this cake?"

Zach's chuckle should have been a warning before he replied, "Chocolate climax."

Chapter Thirteen

Ginna deemed the afternoon perfect for a backyard barbecue. Zach presided over the grill while the twins played with Casper.

Emma's squeals ripped through the air as she ran around the yard with Casper chasing her. She hopped a few steps away and tossed the ball she held into the air. Casper leaped up and caught it in his mouth.

Emma squealed again and ran over to the dog, wrapping her arms around his neck. Casper stood quietly, stoically accepting her attention. Trey joined them, also petting and hugging Casper.

"It's a shame they don't like the dog," Ginna said dryly. She tapped Zach's arm with the beer bottle she held. He turned from his post at the barbecue and accepted the bottle with a kiss on her forehead as a thank-you. She arched an eyebrow. "That's it? I risk my life making that long trip from the house to here under the hot sun to bring you your beer and I get some teeny kiss? The toll's gone up, handsome."

He grinned. "If I did what I wanted to, the kids would be screaming bloody murder and be talking about it to their therapist for the rest of their lives."

"As long as you don't take Trey to a chick flick too

soon, you'll be fine," she said, brushing off his teasing. "How's the chicken doing? Everything else is ready."

He inspected the grilling meat. "It shouldn't be too much longer." His eyes lingered on her face.

"What?" She laughed, a shade of nervousness infecting it. "I have bugs in my hair?" She started to reach up to check her hair, but he grabbed her hand and brought the palm to his mouth.

"Have I told you how beautiful you are?" he murmured against her skin.

"Not so far today," she said, smiling up at him. "But please feel free to say it as often as you'd like."

He placed a gentle kiss in the heart of her palm.

"For later," he promised, folding her fingers over the kiss.

"You are so bad." Her eyes danced with laughter.

"That's not what you said a couple nights ago," he reminded her.

"Heat of passion and all that." Ginna waved it off.

"Chicken's ready," he announced, picking up the platter she'd brought out for him.

Ginna turned toward the yard. "Kids, time to wash up for dinner!" she called out.

"Is Casper gonna eat with us, too?" Emma asked, running toward her with Trey in tow.

"He can, can't he?" Trey put in his own appeal.

"He can't sit at the table until his manners get better," Ginna explained, leading the twins into the kitchen.

She set a small stool in front of the kitchen sink so they could clamber up and wash their hands. Once their hands were clean, she gave Emma the paper plates and Trey the flatware to carry outside. She followed them, carrying a bowl of potato salad in one hand and a bowl of potato chips in the other. After setting them down, she returned to the kitchen for the rest of their meal.

She playfully scolded Emma for feeding Casper a piece of her chicken while Trey gloated and declared she was in trouble and he wasn't.

"Eat and you don't have to worry about getting into trouble," Zach told them both.

"I wish we had a dog," Emma said wistfully at Casper, who lay happily at her feet.

"We can have a puppy, can't we, Daddy?" Trey asked.

"When you get older," Zach said, as if he'd said it many times before.

"How much older?" Trey tried to pin him down.

"Older."

"Daddy talk for when he's old enough to take care of a dog," Ginna confided in a mock whisper.

"But you have a dog." Emma looked at Casper as if she wanted to run off with him. The shepherd looked up as if he was aware he was the subject of their conversation.

"And there're times I feel bad when I'm gone and have to leave him alone," Ginna replied.

Emma looked at Ginna with eyes so very like her father's. "Then why don't you get another dog so Casper will have a friend to play with and he wouldn't be lonely?"

"One dog is enough, thank you very much." Ginna cut into her chicken. "Casper takes up enough of the bed as it is."

"He sure does," Zach muttered, earning a censuring frown from Ginna.

"But if you had two dogs, you could give them their own bed," Trey piped up. "Or maybe you need kids to play with Casper so he wouldn't feel lonely," he slyly added.

She shook her head. "If I had two dogs, they'd both want my bed. Dogs have minds of their own. Casper is spoiled. Not as much as some, but he's definitely spoiled. He believes half the bed is his."

"No sh—!" Zach flinched when the pain radiated across his shin from where Ginna kicked it.

Emma shook her finger at her dad. "Daddy! You almost said a bad word."

"And he's very sorry about it," Ginna explained, arching an eyebrow at Zach.

He obediently hung his head in shame. The twins giggled.

"Nana Cathy spoils Casper," Emma announced, using the name Cathy had suggested she and Trey use with the explanation all the children called her that, while Lou was known as Papa Lou. "She makes him special dog biscuits."

Since that first visit, the twins had been back to the Walker home several times and now considered it their home away from home. Trey gloried in learning all about engines from Lou and Theo, while Emma enjoyed her time in the kitchen with Cathy. Zach told Ginna that he was waiting for the twins to announce they were moving out there. Especially after the family cat gave birth to kittens. Even the prospect of attending kindergarten in a few months wasn't as exciting as going out to Nana Cathy and Papa Lou's for a day of fun.

Zach was amazed that the older couple had taken two more children into their hearts so easily.

Going there, becoming part of the group, showed him what it was like in a large family. Lucie and Nick were always invited and had gone a couple times.

After the children ate, they ran back to the plastic wading pool Ginna had set in the middle of the lawn.

"Make sure Casper stays out of the pool!" Ginna called after them.

"We will!" Trey yelled back, jumping in it himself and sending sprays of water everywhere.

"Are you sure you want that out there?" Zach asked, watching the children splash each other.

"They love it," she replied. "And it will remain in one piece as long as Casper stays out of it. Not easy for him to do, since he loves water." She used her feet to scoot one of the other chairs over in front of her so she could prop her feet on the seat. She picked up her glass of iced tea and sipped it. "It's such a beautiful day."

"We could have gone out for dinner somewhere," he said. "That way you wouldn't have had to go to so much trouble."

Ginna shook her head. "The kids wouldn't have had as much fun in a restaurant. Here, we can all relax." She moved one leg and tickled his leg with her toes. "See?" She lifted her brows in a comical manner.

"I just wish I could stay the night."

"Poor baby," she cooed. She started laughing. "Look at you! Right now, you look just like Trey when you told him he didn't need that model car he found."

"I miss my car when I'm not with it." He put on a forlorn face.

She continued running her toes up and down his bare leg, moving farther upward with each sweep of her toes.

"What do you miss the most about your precious car?" she asked in a low voice.

He looked upward as he considered his answer.

"Well, the headlights are always nice, but it's the tires I like the most."

"I should have known you were a tire man," Ginna said with a heavy sigh. "I bet you like the fancy rims, too."

"It depends." He cocked his head to one side, considering her. "A nice peppy engine."

"At least you didn't say perky."

He held up a hand. "Smooth lines, nice paint job, maybe one of the European models," he mused.

She inched her sunglasses down her nose so she could glare at him. "European model? I don't think so."

He grinned. "Not even one with a snazzy tailpipe?"

"I'll have Dad find you a nice clunky truck."

Zach feigned sorrow. "And here I thought I'd finally get the car of my dreams."

"Ginna! Come play with us!" Emma shouted.

"I'll be over there in a little while," she called back. "Right now, I'm explaining cars to your dad."

"Daddy plays Matchbox cars with me," Trey offered.

Ginna looked at Zach with amused sympathy. "Poor baby having to settle for a substitute."

When the twins fell asleep, Ginna suggested putting them in the guest room, saying the queen-size bed was more than big enough for the two of them.

Zach was worried about the sheets, since the kids hadn't had their baths that evening and were dirty from their time outside. She assured him it was fine. The sheets could always be washed.

Ginna was tucking the sheet around Emma when the little girl opened her eyes.

"I love you, Ginna," she whispered.

She smiled. "I love you too, sweetie."

Emma held up her arms and Ginna leaned down for a hug.

"I wish you were my mommy," she whispered in her ear. "Casper could come to our house, too."

Ginna's smile slipped a notch. "I see what you're doing. You just want my dog," she teased.

Emma shook her head. "No, I want you, but I wouldn't mind if Casper lived with us, too." She yawned and closed her eyes. Within seconds she was fast asleep.

Ginna checked the covers around the sleeping Trey and kissed him on the forehead. Casper looked up from his post on the end of the bed. She patted him on the head and left the room.

With her emotions running the way they were, she stopped in the bathroom first. A cold cloth to her eyes kept the tears at bay, but she could still feel the roll and pitch inside her body. She sat down on the commode and fought to keep her composure. After a few minutes she felt better. She checked herself in the mirror, applied a light touch of lipstick and blush for color and walked out to the family room, where she found Zach watching television. He looked up and smiled at her.

"A night for the record books. They went to sleep without any excuses to stay up," he said.

"It would be tempting to use them as hostages to keep you here all night." She curled up on the couch next to him.

Zach draped his arm around her as she laid her head on his chest, one arm curved around his waist. He turned down the volume on the television. They sat quietly, his fingers combing through her hair soothingly.

"With Casper in there, they won't be able to move a muscle without him alerting us. He takes his job as bodyguard very seriously."

"Which gets his attention off me. I'm very grateful

to them for that. I thought I'd be bribing him with bones for a long time to come.''

Ginna's hand crept under the hem of his polo shirt and flattened against the warm contours of his chest.

The urge to talk wasn't there. Their shared silences were always comfortable. Just as they were tonight.

If they talked, would the conversation turn more personal than usual? Ginna wondered.

Their time together was precious to her. She saw Zach three or four times a week. Most of the time the twins were with him. She never minded, because she loved them. She didn't want to think about using the L-word with the twins, because then she'd have to admit to herself that she was in love with Zach.

That was something she couldn't allow, because in the end it would hurt too much.

She was prejudiced. Zach was the perfect father. The twins were well behaved, well adjusted and wonderful to be around.

But no matter how Zach felt about her, she knew the time would come when he would realize he wanted more. Part of that more would involve children. Someone like him deserved a lot of children. She saw how he was with all the kids at her parents' place. Zach was a man who deserved lots of children just like her father.

When she stopped and thought about it, she realized he was a lot like Brian and Jeff. Loyal to his woman and his children.

Except, in the long run, she couldn't be his woman. She didn't want him to ever regret not having more children because he'd chosen her.

''Why so quiet?'' Zach brushed her hair from her cheek. His fingertips lingered against her skin.

''No reason. I'm just so comfortable.'' She shifted

slightly, enjoying the feel of his bare skin against her palm. She moved her face so she could inhale the musky scent of his skin. "You're like a nice lumpy teddy bear."

"Lumpy?" He sounded offended. "You couldn't come up with a better word to describe my body?"

"I like teddy bears," she said sleepily. "They're warm and comfortable and make me feel safe."

"And here I thought I was nothing more than a sex toy to you."

She raised her head up enough to smile at him. "I do have to say you are a wonderful toy."

He found the hem of her tank top and slid his hand under the soft cotton.

"You had to know that wearing this and no bra today would drive me crazy." He proved his statement as his hand moved over her rib cage.

"And here I thought you were a tire man."

"I am," Zach said promptly. "And damn proud of it."

Ginna branded his bare chest with her smile.

"That's for being such a wonderful man," she told him. Then she struck fast as lightning, blowing a raspberry against his chest. "And that's for having the nerve to compare me to a car."

"Oh, really?" He sprung equally fast, tickling her in every vulnerable spot.

"Zach!" She laughed, pulling him, then losing her balance so that they both fell off the couch. They rolled around on the carpet in a battle to see who would give up first.

In the end Ginna cried uncle. She was laughing so hard she couldn't breathe. Zach sat up and brought her upright.

''See what happens when you play too hard?'' he chided.

A low woof caught their attention. Casper stood in the doorway looking at them as if to say, *You'll wake the twins!*

''Sorry, we'll be more quiet,'' Ginna told the dog.

The dog turned and left. A moment later they heard a soft thump that told them he'd jumped back on the guest-room bed.

Ginna smothered her giggle.

''First time I've been scolded by a dog,'' Zach said.

''He takes his baby-sitting duties very seriously,'' she explained. Twisting her body, she suddenly pushed him backward until he lay on the carpet. She leaned over him with her hands planted on either side of his head. ''But if we're very quiet...'' she whispered.

''Just how quiet can you be?'' he whispered back.

She leaned down, skimmed his lips with her own. ''Quiet as a mouse.'' She grazed his lips again until they parted. She touched the tip of her tongue to his.

At the same time, Zach pulled her down on top of him, their legs tangling. He wrapped a hand around the back of her head and rolled them over so that he now lay over her. He lowered his head and kissed her deeply. They ran their hands over each other, reacquainting themselves with every curve, every line, every sensitive inch of skin that responded to the lightest of touches. Even a feathery touch ignited a firestorm neither expected.

Shirts were yanked up, pants yanked down. It was swift and silent. A coupling they were desperate for. The need to connect in the most elemental way.

When Ginna opened her mouth to cry out Zach's

name, he swallowed her cry with his mouth. When she climaxed, he followed her.

"I don't care what you say, you're a succubus," he said once he could talk. "You attack me and take my vitality. One morning I'm going to wake up and find myself a withered old man."

"No way I'd do that to you. I like you the way you are." She gave a sigh as she lay back with her eyes closed. Her hair was mussed, lips swollen and rosy, skin flushed.

"I already feel safer." He leaned over and pulled down her shirt. "Nice headlights."

Ginna laughed and groaned at the same time.

"I'm hungry. Can I have some more cake?"

They looked up, quickly scrambling to make sure their clothing was at least partially put back to rights. Trey stood in the doorway, looking bleary-eyed.

Zach turned to Ginna. "Real life intrudes," he said softly with a hint of regret.

She touched his cheek. "At least he didn't show up five minutes ago." She stood up. "Since it's pretty late for cake, how about a cup of hot chocolate with baby marshmallows in it?" she asked.

Trey's face lit up. "Yeah!"

"Then let's go make some hot chocolate, and if your daddy says please, we'll make him a cup, too," she confided, holding out her arms. The little boy leaped up, wrapping his legs around her waist. She kissed him on the nose as she carried him to the kitchen.

As she turned on the light, she realized just how natural it felt to bring a little boy in here and fix him a cup of hot chocolate.

All those feelings she feared were rolling in full force.

"Can I have hot chocolate, too?" Emma walked in, looking as heavy-eyed as her brother.

"Of course." Ginna smiled as she guided the children to the table.

When Zach joined them a few minutes later, they sat around the table and drank hot chocolate.

It should have been a happy time for Ginna.

So why did she feel like crying?

"SO HOW ARE THINGS going? Really?" Nora pressed as she and Ginna were seated at a restaurant the next day for lunch.

Since both had a couple of free hours, they decided to enjoy a leisurely lunch and some shopping.

Ginna hadn't expected Nora to see her confusion. She should have known better.

"I'm fine. You know how busy it's been lately. Except for today." She managed to chuckle. "Dad's excited because he has a Tucker to work on. Mom's taking yoga along with her kickboxing class. I don't know where she finds the time to do all she does. Then Jeff and Abby…" Her voice fell off.

Nora shook her head. "Zach, Emma, Trey." She stated each name. "They're obviously a team. And you did it right, Gin. You not only fell in love with the man, but with his kids, too. And they obviously love you. How great is that? Judging from the expression on your face, it's obviously not as great as it should be," she answered her own question. "Tell Aunt Nora."

Ginna toyed with her iced tea.

"Emma told me she wishes I was her mother," she said. Her laughter came out strangled. "She said Casper can live with them, too." She picked up her purse and dug through the contents.

"Here." Nora handed her a handkerchief. "Why did I know this would come in handy?" she muttered. "Gin, you said yourself that he knows all about you. He's spent time with your family and survived. That alone is a biggie. Each time I've seen that man he looks at you the way I look at Keanu Reeves. Except, unlike me, his is more than major lust. The man is so in love with you that it's turned into a blinding aura. Do you know how lucky you are?"

Ginna nodded. "But it won't work." She started crying. She finally took a deep breath. She carefully wiped her eyes, then blew her nose. "I'm sorry. We go out for lunch and I get a crying jag."

"Oh, Gin, how long have you held this in?" Nora asked, watching her sip her iced tea.

"Probably too long." She eyed the Chinese chicken salad she'd ordered. Considering how she had been looking forward to it, she now didn't even want to look at it. She reached for her roll and tore it into bits. "Because Zach didn't tell me right away about the kids, I wanted to be mad at him, but I couldn't. After all, wasn't it better for me to date a man who already had children? Then he wouldn't start thinking I was a bad deal since I couldn't have them. Right?"

"You were never a bad deal," Nora said forcefully. "Denny was the bad deal. You've gone past that. You lucked out finding the absolutely most perfect guy in the world. I wouldn't be surprised if he asks you to marry him. When that happens, you will not think of any idiotic arguments as to why you can't marry him. Do you hear me? You will smile, tell him what a surprise and say yes, because deep down that's what you want."

Ginna stared at her friend. "Where did this aggressive

side to you come from? You used to be such a calm levelheaded person.''

''That was before my best friend decided to do something stupid. And you are, aren't you? You're going to do something stupid.'' Nora took the second roll out of Ginna's hands before she could demolish it, too. She split it open and buttered it. ''Eat your salad,'' she ordered.

Ginna's grin was faint but there. ''Yes, Mother.'' She picked up her fork.

''And the rest of my lecture? You did hear it, right?''

''Yes.''

''And?'' Nora waved her fork in front of Ginna's face.

''He hasn't asked me yet,'' Ginna argued.

''But he will.'' Nora worked on her own salad. ''I really should hate you. Instead, I'm giving up men. It will be much easier on the nerves. A so-called nice guy asks me out, I accept, and next thing I know he's a total loser. I've decided I can't do this anymore. You got the last good one. Hang on to him, because if you do something stupid such as throw him back, I will move in so fast your head will spin. No ruffly bridesmaid dresses, okay? And you know I'm always right.'' She smirked.

Ginna looked at her friend. ''We really need to discuss what sympathy means, because you have completely lost the concept.''

ZACH LOOKED at the contract lying in front of him. His agent had assured him it was a great deal. Zach looked at the numbers and knew he was right.

He had almost four years' worth of columns to work with. The publisher liked the idea of writing the book from a father's perspective from day one. All the hopes and worries he went through.

It would be a new beginning for him. Expanding the columns, recalling the twins from day one. From that first time he held them in his arms.

Trey's first word turning out to be a mangled version of Emma's name.

Emma learning to walk by holding her hands straight out from her sides to keep her balance. Her gurgled laughter as she succeeded.

Trey falling out of a swing and breaking his arm. Zach comforting the crying boy as he drove at breakneck speed to the hospital.

The day at the park when Emma was stung by a bee. His fear when she went into shock. A horrible way to find out his daughter was allergic to bee stings. His cold fear as he sat in the hospital emergency room waiting for word that his little girl was all right.

Then there was their first day of preschool. How badly he wanted to keep them home with him because he knew they would be safe as long as they were with him. And the awareness that the only way they could grow as individuals was to go out into the world.

It still hurt like hell.

And now kindergarten loomed in their future. The beginning of a future that fate mapped out for them. It wouldn't be long before they left him behind.

The publisher even hinted another book could be in the offing if this one did well.

He'd always enjoyed his work. It paid well enough for him to remain home with the twins during their formative years.

But now they were growing. Emma's insistence on a mother was more than a child's wish.

A teenage Trey he could handle. He knew what teenage boys thought and did. But girls were still a mystery.

Growing up with Lucie showed him what happens with teenage girls. Lucie, the adolescent girl, had been an education he doubted he'd ever forget. But dealing with his sister was totally different than dealing with his daughter.

Ginna would know what to do. Cathy and Lou were perfect grandparent material.

Zach loved his parents, but they didn't like to think of themselves as grandparents. His father didn't look at Nick's intelligence. He preferred lecturing Lucie that if she didn't spoil the boy, he wouldn't get into trouble. Zach knew differently. Nick was a boy who needed someone to keep him on track. Zach did what he could, but he was only just an uncle.

Zach and Lucie's parents flew out to visit once a year, spent time with the grandchildren and happily returned them to their parents.

His mother wouldn't have dreamed of spending the morning teaching Emma to bake cookies and muffins. And his father wouldn't have spent hours patiently answering Trey's numerous questions on how an engine worked. Or allowed Nick to take a watch apart so he could see if he could put it back together again.

Cathy and Lou, who weren't even blood relatives, did that and more.

If Zach wasn't careful, Ginna would think he loved her for her parents.

He loved Ginna.

That was a given. Maybe he'd fallen in love with her the first moment he saw her while she confidently informed him the seat was hers. Or when she called him her hero. Or the first time they made love. Or maybe he'd fallen in love with her when she'd so easily accepted Emma and Trey. Or just all those times they were together, content to be wrapped in each other's arms.

He picked up the phone and tapped out a number.

"Lucie Donner."

"You planned it all from the beginning, didn't you?" he said without any preamble.

She didn't pretend not to know what he was talking about.

"I told you before. You needed a vacation and Ginna was getting ready to take one. I got a great deal."

"Sure you did. Two people, one seat."

"That was trickier and I don't intend to get anyone in trouble," she said firmly. "What brought all this up again?"

"Maybe the realization that my sister went above and beyond the call of duty to give me something very special." His voice softened. "I guess I really owe you."

"Wow," she said. "All this brotherly love. I really like it. Does this mean what I think it does?"

"That you're a great sister and I love you?"

"Well, that's a given," she said, exasperated with his teasing. "What I'm talking about is you asking Ginna to marry you. She's perfect for you. Besides, I think if the two of you broke up, the kids would insist on going with her."

"You're probably right about that," he replied. "And, yes, I am thinking about proposing to her."

"Yes!"

He winced and held the phone away from his ear before her shrieks of joy shattered his eardrum.

"It's a good thing I have two ears, Luce," he grumbled, "because I just lost the hearing in one of them."

"You name the day and I will take the kids so you can have all the time you need," she promised.

"Let me figure this out first," he told her. "And I don't want you to say one word to Ginna."

"I won't," she vowed. "Just don't waste any time, okay?"

Zach hung up and turned back to the contract. With a grin splitting his face, he signed his name and slid it into an envelope.

One part of his new life was beginning.

Now to get on to the next and most important part of it.

Chapter Fourteen

"When you said we were going out for an elegant dinner, you weren't kidding." Ginna looked at her surroundings with interest. She turned back to Zach. "This is beautiful." She picked up the red rose with its bud just beginning to bloom. The thorns had been carefully clipped away to protect against cuts. She brought it to her nose. The delicate scent tickled her nostrils. Proof it hadn't been grown in a hothouse.

"The perfect background for you," Zach said gallantly. It had been several weeks since the contract had been finalized and he wanted them to be somewhere special when he gave her the good news.

She smiled. "And you in a suit." She openly admired him in the charcoal suit, light-blue shirt and darker-blue tie. "My, my, Mr. Stone, you do clean up good. I am impressed." And glad she'd worn one of her favorite dresses. A red gown with a draped neckline and narrow sequined straps while the skirt fluttered down to her calves in handkerchief points. Nora had done her hair, pulling it up on top of her head in a cluster of curls that looked tousled but had been carefully arranged. Faint hints of glitter in the curls caught the light. Diamond drop earrings that had belonged to her grandmother twinkled each time she turned her head.

"I thought we'd do some celebrating tonight," Zach explained. He leaned back as the wine steward brought over the bottle of champagne he'd ordered. He waited as some was poured into his glass and he sampled it. He nodded his approval, then waited until they were alone again. "The book deal for my column has been finalized, and the contract has been signed and sent back to my agent."

Her face lit up with joy. "Oh, Zach!" She reached across the table and took his hand in hers. "I'm so happy for you. Your columns are wonderful and really need to be shared with a large audience. I can't wait to see the final product."

He toyed with the stem of his champagne glass. "It's going to be a hell of a lot more work than I've done before," he admitted. "I haven't even started writing it, and I'm already scared to death."

"No reason for you to be. All you need to do is read your old columns. You'll know just what you want to write," she assured him. "Something you'd forgotten. Or look at pictures of Emma and Trey to jog the memory banks. No wonder you wanted to celebrate."

"Part of the reason, yes," he murmured.

Ginna lifted her glass. "Here's to a bestselling book on single fathers."

He gently tapped her glass with his own.

Ginna was always more excited by others' accomplishments than any of her own. She was always happiest cheering someone else on.

She knew Zach and his agent had been working on the book deal for some time. Now it had been signed and sealed. She was pleased he wanted to share the moment with her.

She sipped her champagne.

Ginna couldn't help it. She oohed and aahed over each course served with a dramatic flourish by their waiter, who spoke with a French accent that had to be authentic.

"Zach, please do not take this the wrong way," she said softly when she felt confident their waiter was out of earshot. "Since my menu didn't show any prices, I can only assume this dinner is going to cost you a small fortune. You could probably have taken the kids to Disneyland for the weekend."

"They'll get Disneyland," he assured her. "This is Disneyland for the grown-ups. I just wish I'd thought of a limousine to complete the picture. And don't worry about it," he said. "I'm a big-name author now, remember?"

She laughed and returned to her meal, which she swore melted in her mouth.

She didn't leave one crumb of the flourless chocolate cake topped with raspberry sauce that she had for dessert.

"You can bring me here anytime," she said.

"I'll start saving my pennies now." He grinned.

Ginna adjusted her red lacy shawl as they walked out of the restaurant. Zach handed his ticket stub to the valet, who left them to retrieve his vehicle.

"We have to go to the beach," she told him as he drove out of the parking lot.

"We do?" He was amused by her demand.

"Yes," she said firmly. "You can take off your coat and tie, open your collar and take off your shoes and socks. And we'll dance on the sand."

He glanced around and made a quick, and illegal, U-turn.

"You're right. We do need to go to the beach."

"Perfect," Ginna pronounced as they walked along the water's edge. Zach left his coat, tie, shoes and socks in the SUV, along with Ginna's shoes. He rolled up his pant legs before they stepped onto the sand. She waved her hand in the direction of the ocean where the moon seemed to hang from the middle of the sky. Faint sounds of music could be heard coming from a restaurant a short distance away.

She turned around and held up her arms, stepping into Zach's embrace.

"Just like that first night," she said as he swung her around.

"Same ocean. Same us."

They continued dancing even when the music stopped. When they slowed, Zach lowered his head and kissed her.

"I wanted you to have a special evening," he said.

She looked up at him with a face that didn't need the light of the moon to show it was glowing. Her smile said it all.

"And I have. But then, every evening with you is special," she said sincerely.

"I like the idea of spending every evening with you," Zach said softly, keeping her in his arms. "I'd planned on doing this during dinner. In your champagne or hidden in your dessert. But then I had this fear you'd swallow it and we'd end in the emergency room. Not so romantic that way." He reached into his pants pocket and pulled out a small velvet box. He opened it and drew out a ring. "Marry me, Ginna. Marry me and I will share all that I have with you. Marry me and I will love you beyond forever.''

She didn't need to search his face to know he spoke the truth. She heard it in his voice. Sensed it in his very stance.

She swallowed because the words wouldn't come. As the silence lengthened between them, she watched the hope leave Zach's eyes and face.

''You—'' she licked her lips ''—know everything about me.''

''If you mean that you can't have children, yes, but I'm not Denny,'' he reminded her. ''Even if I didn't have Emma and Trey, it wouldn't matter. I love you, not whether you're capable of childbearing or not. What's important is our being together.''

She was afraid she would cry.

''The time will come when you'll want more children,'' she said desperately, then shook her head when he opened his mouth. ''Don't argue with me. You can't honestly know that you won't want more.''

''Two are plenty,'' he told her. ''If we decide to adopt, great, we'll adopt. I'll still be working from home, so it's not as if I'd expect you to be a stay-at-home mom. I know how much you enjoy your work. I want us to be together, Gin.''

''It's easy for you to say that now!'' she cried, backing away from him. ''Denny said it and then he decided he wanted children. His own.''

Zach didn't move. He watched her face under the pearly glow of the moon. Wordlessly he put the ring back in the box and replaced it in his pocket.

''I'll take you home now,'' he said quietly.

Ginna didn't say a word as they walked back to the beach's parking lot.

She wanted to weep at the impersonality of his touch as he helped her into the vehicle.

The silence between them during the drive back to her house was charged with sadness, instead of joy.

The moment she had her front door unlocked and pushed open, he turned to walk away.

"Zach." She touched his arm to stop his retreat. "Please, listen to me. I love you so much it hurts. When you asked me to marry you, there was nothing I wanted to say more than yes."

"But you didn't." His expression was as harsh as his words.

"Because we both need to be sure," she insisted.

Zach shook his head. "I am sure, Ginna. I've never been more sure of anything. I love you and I want you for my wife. But I guess until you get over your fears, that won't be possible. Just remember something. Other than that time in the very beginning, I have never lied to you. Maybe if you think about it, you'll realize all that's holding us back is you."

He left without kissing her or even touching her.

Ginna went inside and closed the door. She could hear the sound of Zach's SUV driving away.

Now the tears began to flow. She slid down the door's surface until she sat on the tile floor. She was so lost in her misery that she was barely aware of Casper whining and licking her face. Seeing how upset his mistress was, he lay down beside her and nuzzled her hand, finally settling his head in her lap by way of comfort.

She had no idea how long she sat there crying. Not that it mattered.

In the space of a few minutes she'd tossed away everything that mattered to her.

She could tell herself from now until doomsday that

what she did was right. That the time would come when Zach would thank her for this.

But all her mentally detailing why she couldn't accept his proposal didn't make her feel any better.

DAMMIT, IT WASN'T supposed to happen that way!

The crying he expected, the refusal hovering on her lips he didn't. He thought she'd accept his ring and they would go back to her house for further celebration.

Didn't she know him by now? She had to know he'd never do anything to hurt her.

Zach alternated between frustration and anger.

He hadn't just popped the question on a whim. He'd thought about it for some time. What it would mean for Emma and Trey. He knew they both would have been delighted to have Ginna for a mother.

He knew her worries about her inability to have children. He also tried to understand why she would hesitate making a lasting commitment. But he thought she'd gone past that by now.

She should know it didn't matter to him. What he loved was the woman she was. The woman who was so open and caring. Who shared her family. Who loved his kids as much as he did.

He gripped the steering wheel until his knuckles whitened. He had no idea where he was going. He just knew he wasn't going home. Lucie had the twins until tomorrow afternoon, so it wasn't as if he had to be back at a certain time.

It wasn't until he stopped before a low building with lights blazing inside that he realized his subconscious had ideas of its own.

Band music with some additional noises echoed off the garage's metal walls as he walked inside.

Lou Walker looked up and smiled. If he found the sight of Zach in wrinkled suit pants and dress shirt odd, he gave no indication.

"There's coffee on the counter." He jerked his head to one side.

"Thanks." Zach filled a heavy ceramic mug and walked back to a car front seat and sat down. The hot liquid seared his throat while the caffeine zapped straight to his brain.

"So what's with the fancy clothing?" Lou asked as he made minute adjustments to a carburetor.

"I signed a book deal and I took Ginna to Chez Louis," Zach said glumly.

The older man whistled under his breath. "I took Cathy there for our anniversary two years ago. I thought about all the parts I could have bought for what I spent that night. Then I looked at Cathy's face and I knew it was worth it." He glanced at Zach. "I guess it wasn't as memorable for you."

"I asked Ginna to marry me," Zach said glumly. "She turned me down."

Lou looked surprised. "From your face alone, I would have figured she hadn't said yes. If she had, you wouldn't be sitting here with your jaw hanging on the ground. She at least give you a reason? Considering the way you two act when you're together, temporary insanity comes to mind."

"She thinks I'm going to want more kids." Zach snorted. "Hell, mine are only four years old and I'm already turning gray. I want to marry *her*. Why can't she understand that?"

"Maybe because Denny, may he go directly to hell, did a number on her before she got smart and filed for divorce." Lou put down his tools and wiped his hands on a greasy rag. He went over to the coffeemaker and poured himself a cup. "He used some pretty nasty words. Defective. Barren. Not a complete woman."

"I'm surprised she didn't do a little surgery on him," Zach said savagely.

"The boys wanted to do some pounding on him. But I think she got her revenge when she took him to court and won. Not to mention she showed a hefty viewing audience just what kind of man he is." Lou sipped his coffee. "Son, if you're coming to me for advice about my daughter, you've come to a dry hole. I haven't been able to figure my girls out since they were five."

Zach lifted his face. "I just want you to know I'm not giving up on her."

Lou smiled. "I didn't think you would. I saw how things were that first time you all came out. We won't give up on you, either. Trey's got the makings of a good mechanic. I don't intend to lose him. Just don't get scared off when Cathy starts planning the wedding as the event of the millennium. There's nothing that woman likes better than giving parties."

Zach cocked his head to one side, listening to the lyrics coming from a radio. "What kind of music is that?"

Lou grinned. "Spike Jones," he announced fondly. "Best way to hear him is good and loud. Since there's no one around for some distance, I can keep it as loud as I want. Cathy prefers I play it out here." He set his mug down and returned to his task. "So why don't you tell me how you plan to woo my daughter into saying yes?"

Zach looked around the garage. Three cars were in various stages of renovation.

"I once compared her to a car," he mused.

Lou chuckled. "It used to be we compared them to pearls, the sea and the moon. Cars I could have handled with my eyes closed. Speaking as someone who's been through the wars, so to speak, I'd like to suggest you go with something more romantic."

Zach's eyes had already gotten a faraway look.

The hours passed as he spoke and Lou listened. By the time Zach left the garage he felt a great deal lighter in spirit.

HOW COULD TWO different tests say two different things?

Ginna wanted to scream.

It was bad enough she felt she had to resort to these measures. Except she was four days late. She who was always as reliable as a Swiss watch.

"Gin, are you okay?" Nora asked from the other side of the door.

Ginna panicked. "Fine." She gathered up the materials and was stuffing them into the trash can.

"I'm coming in because I don't believe you," her friend warned.

Ginna barely got the boxes jammed in the basket when Nora stepped inside. Her gaze immediately zeroed in on what she was doing. She walked over to the trash can and looked at the boxes. Shock rippled across her face as she looked at Ginna.

"Are you—?"

"I can't be!" Ginna snapped. She felt as if she was about to cry.

Nora picked up one of the boxes. "You must think so if you were doing this."

"One said yes. One said no."

Nora pushed them back down into the trash. "Come

on.'' She dragged her out to the lounge. Mercifully it was empty. ''Tell me what happened,'' she ordered.

Ginna told her everything.

''You did *what?*'' Nora looked as if she wanted to strangle her.

''I don't need this,'' Ginna warned.

Nora's eyes flashed with fury. ''I spent two hours fixing your hair,'' she practically spat. ''We took another hour deciding between your red dress and basic black. I knew it. I knew he was going to propose and I expected you to come in here wearing a ring. Instead, you walk in looking as if your last friend died. There is no way I'm dying before I have the chance to kill you,'' she threatened between clenched teeth. ''Not to mention your giving yourself a pregnancy test.''

Ginna rubbed her forehead. ''Don't yell,'' she whined. ''I already have a headache.''

Nora was relentless. ''You always said any man you fell in love with wouldn't want to marry you because you couldn't have kids. So you fall in love with a man who already has kids. He tells you he only wants you. And you throw it back in his face.'' She shook her head. ''Then you have this fear you might be pregnant?''

''I'm four days late,'' Ginna admitted. ''I didn't even think about it until this morning. I am never late. But I can't have kids, so why is this suddenly happening?''

Nora exhaled a deep breath. ''You've done it, Gin. You have totally lost your mind because of a man and a medical report. What exactly did it say? You absolutely couldn't have children? Gin, there're surgical procedures, medication, acupuncture,'' she said in a rush. ''Didn't the report give you any kind of idea what could be done for you?''

''I tuned the doctor out after he said I couldn't have

children. I pushed the report in the back of my desk drawer,'' Ginna confessed. ''Why read something so depressing?''

''Maybe because it might have offered some hope,'' Nora suggested. ''Pull it out and read it.''

''I've thought of that,'' Ginna said. ''I even pulled the papers out of my desk last night. I didn't bother looking at them. It's probably all medical mumbo jumbo.''

''Gee, here you have a doctor in the family who could explain it all to you.''

Ginna curled her lip. ''You're having way too much fun with this.''

Nora affected a dramatic sigh. ''Yes, I am. You've been the happiest I've seen you in a long time. You can't afford to lose Zach over something like this.''

Ginna picked up her phone.

Nora tracked her movements. ''Are you calling Zach?''

She shook her head. ''I'm not ready for that yet. Besides, I need to have that report interpreted first.''

''And if it still says you can't have children?'' Nora pressed.

Ginna winced at the question she knew was coming. Nora wasn't going to let it go.

''Then I will tell Zach I was wrong in not trusting him, that I love him and if he'll ignore my bout of temporary insanity, I would love to marry him.''

Nora nodded enthusiastically. ''Perfect!''

Luckily Gail could meet Ginna for lunch that day. Ginna made a quick trip home to pick up the report before heading for the restaurant. Without unfolding the pages, she stuffed it into her bag and ran back out of the house.

She made it to the restaurant a few minutes before Gail.

"This is wonderful! We haven't done this in a while." Gail smiled at her, taking the chair across from her. "How are you doing?"

"I've been better," Ginna replied. "First of all, lunch is on me. I need to pick your brain."

"Pick away," Gail said. "But for what?"

Ginna took a deep breath. "Zach asked me to marry him." She held up her hand to stop any congratulations. "I turned him down."

"Turned him down? Why?" Then Gail remembered. "Oh, Ginna."

Ginna shook her head. "He knows and it didn't matter to him."

"But it still matters to you."

Ginna reached into her bag and pulled out a long envelope. "This was the medical report the doctor gave me when he told me the news. I want to know if there's any hope for me. Please?"

Gail took the envelope and opened it. She spread the sheets of paper out in front of her, then pulled out her reading glasses.

Ginna sat uneasily in her chair. It seemed hours as she watched the other woman read the two sheets of paper. When Gail finished, she refolded them and put them back in the envelope. She set it carefully in the middle of the table.

"Did you ever look at these?" she asked.

Ginna shook her head. "The doctor said I couldn't have children. Denny looked them over and said I was—" she coughed "—defective."

"I'd love to get a scalpel on the man," Gail muttered.

"All right, here's the easiest layman's explanation I can give you. It was never you. It was Denny."

She looked confused. "Denny? No, he was fine."

Gail muttered a few uncomplimentary words about Ginna's ex-husband. "He lied," she said flatly. "You're not sterile, Ginna."

"But Denny got his girlfriend pregnant," she argued. "Twice!"

"The reason you couldn't get pregnant is very simple. You're allergic to Denny's sperm," Gail explained.

Unfortunately Ginna was sipping her iced tea when Gail made her pronouncement. She immediately choked, spraying iced tea everywhere. She grabbed her napkin and dabbed at her lips.

"Too bad you didn't read it. You were lucky—it was written in very clear language. Not Latin."

"I'm choking and you're laughing!" Ginna wheezed.

"You're not choking to the extent you require medical care," Gail said serenely. Her lips still curved upward. "When you think about it, you have to love the diagnosis. Brian told me what an idiot Denny was. Isn't it wonderful your eggs were smart enough to reject his sperm? I just bet that won't happen with Zach."

Which brought on another choking fit. Ginna covered her mouth with her napkin.

"Now what? I give you good news and you try to swallow your tongue?" Gail asked, now looking concerned.

"We never..." She kept coughing. "There was no reason for..."

Gail's eyes widened. "Could you be...?"

Ginna looked wildly around as she did some mental figuring. "I thought I was. I even tried two of those tests this morning. One said yes and one said no. I'm four

days late and I'm never late. Maybe it's just all nerves.
Or I'm allergic to Zach's sperm, too.''

"I don't think you have anything to worry about. He
looks like the type with extra-strength sperm," Gail told
her. "Look at it this way. Denny didn't want to admit
he had wimpy sperm." She grinned. "Don't worry.
We'll go by my office after lunch. We'll run a test
there.''

"Ma'am, are you all right?" The waitress stopped by
the table, looking at Ginna, who was still wheezing.

"She's fine. She just realized she might be pregnant,"
Gail told her. She glanced at the menu. "What's your
most expensive item?"

THE MINUTE SHE ENTERED the salon, Ginna knew something was up. It wasn't just the way every occupant was
looking at her. Or that CeCe, the owner, was standing
in the rear of the salon with a knowing smile on her lips.

"Did I win the lottery?" she asked.

She already felt loads better. Especially since she'd
made a copy of the doctor's report, underlined the statement pertaining to her allergy to Denny's sperm and
mailed the report to him.

"Ginna," CeCe said in her musical accented voice.
"While you were gone, a gift was delivered for you."

Ginna automatically looked toward her station. No
flowers. No basket of fruit. Not even a candy box.

"Your gift is in the back," CeCe explained, turning
around and heading for the rear of the salon.

The minute she stepped into the lounge she knew just
what her gift was.

A large gift-wrapped box sat on the table and chairs.
The first box revealed a license-plate frame. *Zach loves
Ginna* was framed with small red hearts.

Ginna burst into tears.

CeCe immediately put her arm around her and steered her to one of the chairs. She plucked the card out of Ginna's nerveless fingers and read it.

"A man sends you his declaration of love. He must be very special to do that." She cupped Ginna's chin with her fingertips and lifted her face. "Is this the man who first made you so happy, then made you unhappy?"

"He asked me to marry him." Ginna's chin wobbled.

"You said no, but you wanted to say yes," CeCe stated. "And now he has sent you something that tells you exactly how he feels. Do you think that perhaps you should have said yes to his proposal?"

"I think this means he's not taking no for an answer," Ginna whispered.

"A very good man." CeCe took her handkerchief and carefully dabbed under Ginna's eyes. She clucked her tongue. "I feel you are ready to make things right."

"Gin?" Cheryl walked in carrying a large white box. "It's not big enough for hubcaps." She handed it to Ginna.

Ginna opened the box and looked inside. She set the box on the table and carefully drew out a glass globe.

"A headlight?" Cheryl said.

"More than a headlight." Ginna held it up to show a transparent design painted on the glass. A heart with an arrow through it. *ZS loves GW.*

"The man is unique. Most men would have sent flowers or candy," CeCe said. She smiled. "He wants you to know exactly how he feels. I think this Zach knew just what would melt your heart. And it has, hasn't it?" She patted her cheek. "You need to go see him, Ginna. You must tell him you will be very happy to be his wife."

"I have clients," she argued, still not ready.

CeCe fluttered her hands. "Yes, perhaps you will need the distraction. And we will require the time to take away those red eyes and shiny nose." She put her hands on Ginna's shoulders and turned her around, gently pushing her forward. "Ladies, our Ginna needs some of our magic before she goes to Zach."

"By morning, I'll be fine," Ginna protested.

"Never!" CeCe insisted. "Come, we have preparations to make." She smiled. "We wish Zach to know just how lucky he is."

"I can just tell him," Ginna muttered as Hurricane CeCe herded her out of the room.

Chapter Fifteen

"Why can't I call Ginna?" Emma demanded in a belligerent tone that was unlike her usual sunny self.

"Because she's busy," Zach said wearily. "And don't ask me again."

Emma's expression turned mutinous as she faced her father.

"Did you have a fight with Ginna?"

"What?"

"You heard me," she said with an expression on her face that was reminiscent of Lucie. "You were really happy when you went to dinner with Ginna. But when you picked us up at Aunt Lucie's, you weren't happy anymore. Did you have a fight with her?"

"Why is it always the man's fault?" He wearily rubbed his forehead. "I swear, Em, you're spending way too much time with your aunt Lucie."

Emma looked at him with wide eyes. "Aunt Lucie said you musta done somethin' really bad. Did you do somethin' bad, Daddy?"

Zach swallowed the comment he wanted to make about dear Aunt Lucie's remarks on the subject.

"Ginna's real busy right now," he lied. He hadn't

told Emma and Trey that he wouldn't be seeing Ginna anymore.

Is this what divorce is like? The pain of separation? He remembered the pain he'd felt after Cathy's death and he never wanted to experience that again.

"Daddy?"

Judging from the worried look on her face, she'd been talking to him and he hadn't been listening. All he'd done was sit there wondering what Ginna had thought of his gifts. Would he find them on his front lawn in the morning?

"I'm sorry, Peanut. Maybe Daddy's coming down with a cold," he said with a smile. He kissed her on the forehead.

"Then we'll give you cod-liver oil and kisses like Grandma said she gave you when you were little," she told him.

"The kisses, yes. We'll hold off on the cod-liver oil." He enveloped her in his arms, holding her tightly, as if her touch could take away the pain of losing Ginna.

Why couldn't she have trusted him? He'd vowed he would never do anything to hurt her. Why didn't she accept his words?

He knew one thing. If the headlights and license-plate frame didn't work, he'd sic the twins on her next.

He refused to believe she could withstand them.

Especially Emma when she used her wide-eyed little girl act that always had him giving in to her. Not all the time, but often enough. Where his daughter was concerned, he could be a wuss as a father.

Zach was desperate and it had only been three days.

If it took kidnapping Ginna and dragging her to Las Vegas for a quickie chapel wedding, he would do it.

"Daddy?" Emma patted his cheek to get his attention.

The tip of her tongue appeared as it always did when she was worried. "Everything will be okay. You'll see."

He couldn't help but smile.

THERE MAY HAVE BEEN no jet waiting to whisk her off to Hawaii, but as before, Ginna had been shampooed, moussed and massaged, and her face glowed with an aromatherapy facial. Instead of casual clothing, she wore a silk dress that revealed more than it covered.

Ginna spent the night reading and rereading the medical report. Then she sat back and recalled every moment she'd spent with Zach.

She didn't need anyone to tell her just how wrong she'd been. She was doing a good job of it all by herself.

The next day, under CeCe's supervision, she was given beauty treatments that CeCe insisted would dazzle Zach.

Ginna tried to protest, but the older woman ignored her. Ginna already knew what she had to do. Essentially she wasn't going to waste any time telling him she was wrong. That she should have known better than to doubt him. Then she'd ask him if the proposal was still open. If that didn't work, she wasn't above using the children to change his mind.

During the drive to his house, she ran through various scenarios, then tossed them all out the window.

Instead, she thought about the times they were together. The way he'd comforted her at the beach when she told him about her inability to have children.

All the clues were there and she'd stubbornly ignored them.

She had been a fool. It would serve her right if Zach refused to talk to her. But she was hoping he'd give her a chance.

After she parked at the curb, she sat there for a few moments looking at the house.

The lights she could see glowing through the windows looked inviting. She only hoped they would continue to be inviting for her.

She finally took a deep breath and climbed out of the car.

Knowing the twins would be in bed by now, she knocked on the door, instead of using the doorbell. It was a few moments before she heard footsteps from the other side of the door. She stood back so she would be highlighted by the light next to the door.

She held her breath until she heard the click of the dead bolt and saw the door opening. A grim-faced Zach stood before her.

"I could say I was in the neighborhood, which I know you wouldn't believe," she blurted. "Or I could say you left something at my house, but I don't think that would work, either. So I came by to thank you for my new headlights and license-plate frame. And especially to tell you I was wrong," she whispered.

Zach didn't say anything, but he stood back and opened the door further. As she stepped inside, she could see a light on in the rear of the house.

"I was working," he explained, guiding her to one side. "Would you like something to drink?"

"No, thank you." She perched tensely on the edge of a chair. "Look, you were right. I let the past rule my thoughts. I didn't let go the way I should have. And I didn't trust you. I didn't remember what was important. That you never lied to me." She blinked rapidly. The last thing she wanted was cry. "I'm sorry."

Zach walked over and crouched in front of her. He

pulled a handkerchief out of his pocket and handed it to her.

"Thank you. I seem to be doing that a lot lately." She sniffed and accepted the cotton square. "Crying, that is." She winced when she noticed the dark marks on the white fabric. "I guess I didn't use my waterproof mascara." She balled up the handkerchief.

Zach took her hands in his. "You didn't even give me a chance, Ginna," he said quietly. "Admittedly you didn't scream a resounding no, but you might as well have. I thought we were on the same track."

"We are," she told him. "Unfortunately I took a little side trip into temporary insanity. Blame it on cold medicine I never took. PMS. Anything. But please, can we try this again?" she whispered. "Zachary Michael Stone, Jr., will you marry me?"

"You finally believe me when I say we have two kids and that's enough?" he said, still holding on to her hands. "That I love you and that's all that matters?"

"Yes, I do. Does this mean you'll marry me?" she pleaded.

"No backing out now," he warned her. "Because I'm saying yes, and if you don't go through with it, I'm not above suing you for breach of contract."

She nodded, still sniffing. "I have something else I need to tell you," she said in a small voice that had him thinking of Emma when she'd done something bad.

"There's more?" Now he was really worried. Had something happened in the past three days? No, if it was something serious, Lou would have called him.

"You see, I never read the medical report the doctor gave me," she explained. "I just put it away. But Nora told me I should read it. Since I didn't think I would fully understand all the terms, I asked Gail to lunch and had her read it."

"Okay? And?"

"And—" she drew out the word "—Denny lied to me. I'm not sterile, I'm just allergic to his sperm. But even before I found out, I told Nora I was going to prove to you I came to my senses," she said without taking a breath. "So I'm not here just because I learned I'm not sterile. I'm here because I love you and I don't want to lose you."

Zach's grip on her hands tightened until she yelped.

"You're pregnant?" he asked, stunned by her announcement.

"No! But all those times we never used anything. It could have happened. And don't dare say I could be allergic to yours. No way. No how. We've just been lucky." Her smile grew larger. "Scary, huh?"

"Scary, hell, it's enough to stop my heart." He stood up, pulling her with him. "I should make you as miserable as I've been for the past three days," he muttered, "but dammit, I can't. Not when I've got you here." He covered her mouth, hungrily taking all she had to give. Her knees were starting to buckle when he released her. "I'll be right back." He turned and left the room.

She dropped to the chair before she fell.

When Zach returned, he held the velvet box.

Before she could take a breath, he had the ring out and on her finger.

"I am not giving you a chance to say no," he informed her. "You better tell your mother the wedding will be soon."

"Considering she's been planning one since she met you, I don't think that will be a problem." She threw her arms around him. "Maybe I needed this time of misery to fully appreciate this. And to realize how mistaken I was.'' She peppered his face with kisses. ''I will never doubt you again.''

''You shouldn't have in the beginning,'' he scolded, scooping her up, then sitting down and arranging her in his lap. ''The kids were miserable. Lucie thought I did something wrong. And I was in hell.''

Ginna murmured a few soothing words as she continued kissing him.

''I'll tell them it was my fault,'' she told him. ''Daddy will say I was crazy. Mom will tell me she was glad I came to my senses, and my brothers won't have to beat you up, because no matter what they would have blamed you.''

''I'm glad to hear that.'' All the tension had been erased from his face. A face she loved. She traced its contours with her fingertips.

''The kids will love knowing you're going to be their mother,'' he said.

''Nah, they just want my dog.'' She couldn't stop kissing him. She smiled, aware he wasn't about to argue. ''But that's okay. I'm still getting the best deal.''

He moved his hand up her thigh. ''Damn, I've missed these tires.''

''There've been some things I've missed, too.'' She shifted on his lap.

''Daddy? Ginna!'' A small body launched itself onto Ginna's lap. Zach grunted at the extra weight. ''You came back!'' Emma hugged her tightly.

''Of course I did,'' she said.

''So Daddy didn't do anything wrong?'' Emma asked.

Ginna looked at his face and smiled. ''Daddy did something very right,'' she murmured before she turned to the little girl. "How would you and Trey feel if I became your mom?"

Emma's shrill squeal was her answer.

Zach winced. "Hey, kid, you're going to shatter the windows."

Before Ginna grabbed hold of her, Emma hopped off and ran down the hallway.

"Trey! Trey! Ginna's going to be our mom!"

"I guess that's a yes," Zach said.

Emma soon returned with Trey behind her. He yelled Ginna's name and jumped into her lap to hug her.

"Really?" he asked.

"Really," Ginna confirmed.

"Then Papa Lou and Nana Cathy will really be our papa and nana!"

"You know, we need to celebrate." Ginna felt the adrenaline race through her body. Keeping Trey in her arms, she stood up. "Put on your robes, we're going out for hot-fudge sundaes." She set him down and he ran down the hall after his sister.

Zach laughed. "You're definitely getting them on your side. It's a school night and they're going out in their pajamas."

"We had our champagne. They need their hot-fudge sundaes. Besides, who's going to notice a couple of little kids in their pj's? They can have little sundaes," she replied. "I want to share the celebration with them. Do you mind?" She rested her hands on his chest.

"Keep touching me like that and the kids will have to wait for their sundaes," he warned her.

The kids ran back into the room, not caring that their robes were haphazardly belted. Ginna halted them long enough to straighten the robes and tighten the belts, then she received more hugs.

As they left the house with the chattering twins running ahead of them, Ginna touched Zach's arm. He stopped and looked at her with a question in his eyes.

"What do you think if one of the first invitations we send out goes to the judge who gave me that judgment?" she suggested. "After all, if she hadn't given me the judgment, I wouldn't have been able to afford the trip that Lucie sent me on so I would meet you." She smiled.

Zach looked at her lovingly. He believed her when she said she'd already planned to call him even before she knew the contents of the report.

She just needed to come to terms with herself. He was just grateful it hadn't taken her longer than the three days they'd been apart to know that what they shared was very right.

He smiled. "Just as long as we don't let Lucie think she gets all the credit. Then she'd be insufferable."

Ginna clutched his arm with both hands and leaned her head against his shoulder.

"Not when we explain to her that we would have to give the credit to the flight attendant. She was the one who told you to sit next to me."

"Something tells me if there's a next book, it will be about a woman who swept me off my feet." He watched the twins scramble up and into their child seats.

"You do realize something else, don't you?" she asked.

He shook his head.

"Think about it, Zach. Twins run in both our families." She hugged him tightly, so happy that she couldn't stop herself.

He helped her into the passenger seat. "Something tells me we're going to have to look for a bigger house."

As Zach drove down the road, Ginna alternated her

gaze between him and the twins, who were talking excitedly in the back seat. Mainly arguments as to who Casper would sleep with. Zach glanced her way and smiled. He held out his hand and she took it. Felt the warmth of his skin and the warmth of his love.

Something precious she'd almost tossed away because of past fears.

She made a silent pledge that she wouldn't allow the past to haunt her present or future. No more looking back.

Not when looking forward was giving her so much more.

▼ SILHOUETTE®
SPECIAL EDITION™

AVAILABLE FROM 18TH JULY 2003

THE ROYAL MacALLISTER Joan Elliott Pickart

The Baby Bet: MacAllister's Gifts

For two weeks only, Alice MacAllister and irreverent royal Brent Bardow could laugh, love and ignore the future they'd never have. But she couldn't help wondering what it would be like to be his royal bride...

HIS EXECUTIVE SWEETHEART Christine Rimmer

The Sons of Caitlin Bravo

Celia Tuttle knew that falling madly in love with her boss, Aaron Bravo, was a terrible mistake—she *knew* he'd never marry. Offering her resignation was clearly the solution...but would he let her go?

TALL, DARK AND DIFFICULT Patricia Coughlin

After his accident, daring pilot Major Hollis 'Griff' Griffin no longer cared about anything—except perhaps delectable Rose Davenport. Could she break down the icy barriers around Griff's heart?

WHITE DOVE'S PROMISE Stella Bagwell

The Coltons

Handsome playboy Jared Colton was the town hero, but single mother Kerry was immune to his charm. Rescuing her child caught her attention...but what would he do to keep it?

DRIVE ME WILD Elizabeth Harbison

Grace Bowes' first job interview *ever* was with brooding bachelor Luke Stewart, the man who'd once made her heart beat madly—before she'd married someone else. The man who still made her wonder: what if...?

UNDERCOVER HONEYMOON Leigh Greenwood

Maggie Oliver had an undercover assignment, a pretend honeymoon—with CIA agent Noah Brant, the man who'd once been her lover. Could this deadly charade lead them back to the love they'd lost?

Maitland Maternity

Where the luckiest babies are born!

Cassidy's Kids
by Tara Taylor Quinn

Troublesome twins… A single father…
An old flame…

Sloan Cassidy is a single dad with eighteen-month-old twins and he needs help! He knows one person who could help him, somebody he would love to see again. The trouble is, he hasn't been in touch with her for ten years...

Ellie Maitland has always had a soft spot for children and Sloan's little girls. But everyone knows this gorgeous rancher broke her heart. Everyone that is, except Sloan!

4 FREE

books and a surprise gift!

We would like to take this opportunity to thank you for reading this Silhouette® book by offering you the chance to take FOUR more specially selected titles from the Special Edition™ series absolutely FREE! We're also making this offer to introduce you to the benefits of the Reader Service™—

- ★ FREE home delivery
- ★ FREE gifts and competitions
- ★ FREE monthly Newsletter
- ★ Exclusive Reader Service discount
- ★ Books available before they're in the shops

Accepting these FREE books and gift places you under no obligation to buy, you may cancel at any time, even after receiving your free shipment. Simply complete your details below and return the entire page to the address below. *You don't even need a stamp!*

YES! Please send me 4 free Special Edition books and a surprise gift. I understand that unless you hear from me, I will receive 6 superb new titles every month for just £2.90 each, postage and packing free. I am under no obligation to purchase any books and may cancel my subscription at any time. The free books and gift will be mine to keep in any case.

E3ZEE

Ms/Mrs/Miss/Mr ....Initials................................
BLOCK CAPITALS PLEASE

Surname ....

Address ....

....

....Postcode................................

Send this whole page to:
UK: FREEPOST CN81, Croydon, CR9 3WZ
EIRE: PO Box 4546, Kilcock, County Kildare (stamp required)

Offer valid in UK and Eire only and not available to current Reader Service subscribers to this series. We reserve the right to refuse an application and applicants must be aged 18 years or over. Only one application per household. Terms and prices subject to change without notice. Offer expires 31st October 2003. As a result of this application, you may receive offers from Harlequin Mills & Boon and other carefully selected companies. If you would prefer not to share in this opportunity please write to The Data Manager at the address above.

Silhouette® is a registered trademark used under licence.
Special Edition™ is being used as a trademark.